Miraculous

By Colette Dixon

Publisher: Inspiring Publishers,
P.O. Box 159, Calwell, ACT Australia 2905
Email: publishaspg@gmail.com
http://www.inspiringpublishers.com

A catalogue record for this book is available from the National Library of Australia

National Library of Australia The Prepublication Data Service

Author: Colette Dixon
Title: Miraculous
Genre: Non-fiction

Print ISBN: 978-1-922792-87-7
eBook ISBN: 978-1-922792-88-4

This book is dedicated to my parents Clayton and Carol Dixon who have been role models in Christ and I am ever so grateful to for making me the person I am today.

"Nurture them in the discipline and instruction of the Lord" Ephesians 6:4

The work contained herein has been produced with the intent to provide relevant knowledge and information on the topic, while the author has gone to every extent to furnish up-to-date and true information, the author has made no claims to be an expert on this topic.

Notwithstanding, the reader is asked to do their own research and consult any subject matter experts they deem necessary to ensure the quality and accuracy of the material presented herein.

The data, depictions, events, descriptions, and all other information forthwith are considered to be true, fair, and accurate.

* References are provided at the end of the book.

Table of Contents

Chapter 1

It's In My Fate

For I know the plans I have for you," declares the LORD, "plans to prosper you and not to harm you, plans to give you hope and a future." —Jeremiah 29:11

"A blast of shrill sirens and flashing red lights blocks out everything. My belly tightens, and my eyes again reach to find anyone's kind gaze. My hand squeezed and the knot in my gut loosened".

The Journey

It was a priest's prophecy that sent me from Calcutta, India, to study in Australia. His prophecy entailed that "God was going to work through me". How and why baffled my parents and me. As they blindly trusted the prognosis and packed me off to study in Australia, the enthusiastic me agreed.

Before I tell you my story, I had no intention of wanting to study anywhere in Australia; this country was nowhere on my radar. Only because, after several American teenage soap operas, I had pictured myself entangled in a love triangle, permanently and successfully settled in the United States. But obviously, it didn't go as I intended or planned, and I decided to follow God's plan instead and had to reroute my academic goals to a different country other than the one I had chosen.

"Are you excited?" asked my aunt Caroline. Who had come to visit me along with her son Josh before I had left the country. "Beyond ecstatic", I replied eagerly.

Either way, I was euphoric to be moving across the world to pursue my philosophical journey.

I departed India on the 22nd of January 2007 on route to Thailand mid-way as there were no direct flights to Melbourne.

This was literally the first time I was going to be away from my family, as I had never spent more than a day apart from them. So on that day, I didn't know if I felt excited, nervous, fearful or anxious. The thought of separation from my family, friends and familiar surroundings would not only be challenging, but this transition to a new life in a new country was going to be extremely arduous.

My brother, Calvin, hugged me so tight and said to me, "be safe and take care, don't have too much fun away from us".

I wiped a tear as it rolled down my cheek and replied, "I doubt I'd ever have too much fun".

You see, because I was the eldest sibling, I was also the most overprotected out of the lot. Why? Because it's pretty obvious, most parents are single-minded, and their focus is to keep their firstborn safe, not only physically but also emotionally, by shielding them from all the negativity in the world.

So moving on to the exciting part of my journey, I finally got on the plane and said a little prayer and tried to stay positive but still intrigued by how the Lord would work through me in the days to come.

I took out the novel that I had been reading and set myself up to relax mode, and off we flew.

It was a tiresome 13-hour journey across the Indian Ocean and a mentally draining one too. We had to stop off in Thailand and transit there for a few hours before catching a connecting flight to Melbourne. Though I had a layover in Bangkok, it was not advisable to book a room at a hotel for a few hours. So instead, I made myself feel useful and brazenly walked up to the counter where I exchanged some of my money for Australian dollars so I would be prepared when I got there.

During my endless journey, I pictured the gorgeous city, where I could only imagine being drowned in crowds but not compared to the city I was leaving. Then came the time to board again. The entire 8 hours flew by pretty quick as I was absorbed in the flight's movie selection.

In Calcutta, I felt like a raindrop, protesting to join the ocean. So the feeling of moving to an entirely new country, a spontaneous city, to embark on my scholastic journey, was indescribable, and the energy I felt along with the new country vibe was surreal.

And before I knew it, I looked down on the spectacular city of Melbourne, Australia. I saw a massive city with rivers snaking through it. I arrived in Melbourne at 9.15 pm and knew I already loved this city with every fiber of my being. As I looked out the window, I could see its spacious, tree-lined streets with its precinct buildings. I even spotted one of the city's landmarks, Federation Square, which is adjacent to the Yarra River.

The highways streamed along these; the ocean held it in like an unbreakable barrier. As the buildings became larger during our descent, the land became greener. What a lush country! It seemed the entire continent was covered in grass and trees with water, water everywhere. It is a beautiful city of arched bridges and an extraordinary mix of the old and the new. Contemporary business buildings of steel and glass surrounded old churches of brick and leaded windows and Victorian stations like the Flinders Street railway station built in 1909 backing onto the Yarra River. The hills surrounded the airport as we neared the landing strip and at last touched down.

I felt exhausted, but I pretended not to have a tired bone in my body, so I shrugged off the exhaustion with my enthusiasm.

As I walked out of the airport and got into my ride, the pace in the city was beyond perfect; it looked vibrant, lively, multicultural, and a place I knew I would perfectly fit in.

In the two weeks that led up to my orientation day, I had just experienced a little of the hustle and bustle of the city's stores, food, the renaissance of its old buildings, the city's creativity and quirkiness along with its sheer elegance.

12 February 2007, 6.45pm

Buzzing Buzzing -phone ringing at 6.45 pm Monday evening on the 12th of February

"Yes, Ma, what's up?" I asked

"Just checking to see how you are going and your adrenaline levels as you start your big day tomorrow", my mother said, and before I could even get in a reply, she continued "now follow all instructions on how to get there and back and say the Psalm 91 before you head off".

"Yes, I will, and yes, I will say the Psalm 91 as I say it every morning, as you know", I replied, agitated.

"Just reminding you on top of all the things you need to do before tomorrow", she answered.

"Yup, Got it, okay ma, I'm about to eat dinner and watch an Australian TV show called Neighbors, so I will call you tomorrow to let you know how my day goes" and said my goodbyes with an "I love you" at the end.

I had an early night that night, as the people I was accommodating with usually slept by 8pm, so I went into my room and prepped for an early night too, completing the usual night routine, brushing my teeth, putting on a pair of pj's, saying my nightly prayers and did a little novel reading before I switched off the night lamp near my bed.

13th February 2007, 7 am

My alarm woke me up. I noticed how effortlessly I jumped out of bed as I was excited for the day ahead. I excitedly ate my cereal, completed my morning activity of showering, brushing my teeth, combing my hair, and putting on my best faded jeans with my new top that I recently bought from a night market down the road somewhere.

I dressed carefully that morning. I matched my jeans with a pretty pink top, and a neat pair of ballerina flats that had a bit of white and pink that matched my top. I tied my hair back in a bouncy ponytail and wore tiny star earrings to complete my look.

I patted my face with a powered foundation, used a black eyeliner under my eyes, brushed my eyelashes with my best mascara, applied a little lipgloss and did a fit check in the mirror, smiled, grabbed my backpack and my lunch and headed straight out the door, with a piece of paper of instructions in my hand, that I had to written down the previous night to get to my destination.

Also remembering to repeat the Psalm 91 Bible verse on my way out.

My family and I had studied this Bible verse and easily narrated the entire verse out loud, whenever and wherever.

Psalm 91....

"Whoever dwells in the shelter of the Most
    High will rest in the shadow of the
    Almighty.

I will say of the Lord, "He is my refuge and my
    fortress, my God, in whom I trust."

Surely he will save
    you from the
    fowler's snare

    and from the deadly
    pestilence. He will cover you with
    his feathers,

    and under his wings you will find refuge;
    his faithfulness will be your shield and rampart.

You will not fear the terror of
    night, nor the arrow that flies
    by day,

    nor the pestilence that stalks in the
    darkness, nor the plague that destroys
    at midday.

A thousand may fall at your
    side, ten thousand at your
    right hand, but it will not
    come near you.

You will only observe with your eyes
    and see the punishment of the wicked.

If you say, "The Lord is my refuge,"
    and you make the Most High your
    dwelling, no harm will overtake you,
    no disaster will come near your tent.

For he will command his angels
    concerning you to guard you in all your
    ways;
    they will lift you up in their hands,
    so that you will not strike your foot against a stone.

You will tread on the lion and the cobra;
    you will trample the great lion and the serpent.

"Because he loves me," says the Lord, "I will rescue
    him; I will protect him, for he acknowledges my
    name.

He will call on me, and I will answer
    him; I will be with him in trouble,

    I will deliver him and honor him.
    With long life I will satisfy
    him and show him my
    salvation."

Is it a coincidence that this is the 9-1-1 verse? In whatever troubles we face today, God is the place of refuge where we can run to find safety. He is always our safe place.

I would repeat the words from this verse religiously every morning and still do today, I would say it with my family out loud in front of our devout statue of Mother Mary (that we had and who had been covered with an exuberant gold rosary around her neck), every morning before we began our day.

On my first day of orientation at Monash University, on February 13 2007, the first day of adulting, I was ecstatic to jump into deep water as I knew it would be a mixed feeling of excitement and exhaustion.

I was so fixated on this day and on seeing my campus, which I was about to study in for the first time. I was electrified to see new faces, meet various personalities, and learn more about the subjects I had chosen, on top of everything else I knew I could handle.

It was the 'dee' day I had dreamed about for so long, where I got to attend university abroad and one of the best in the state, mind you!.

I caught the train from Sandown railway station to get off at Berwick railway station, and it took me exactly 22 minutes to get there. I carried a small backpack containing a couple of shredded chicken sandwiches, a drink, a notebook and a pen. For some reason, I left my new Dell laptop at home. I packed my wallet, a phone, my Indian driver's license, and a little bit of Australian currency. I didn't use much of it because I found the ticket machine at the train station too sophisticated. I didn't know how to use it, so I ended up paying $2.10 for a 2-hour train ticket instead of buying a day pass which would have worked out to be cheaper.

As I sat on a seat that was close to the entry/exit door. I gazed out of the train window as it stopped at every station before it got to the main station. I studied every sign post and tried to read all instructions on the platform before it began moving again.

I had finally arrived at my destination, got off the platform, and began walking toward a busy road that led me to the university. I stood at a set of lights and waited for its little pedestrian green man to walk before I crossed the pedestrian crossing.

The campus looked divine; it had a huge logo outside that stood out in a boulder that had been written in bold, its neatly segregated entrance along with its vast car park all aligned.

A thrill rushed through me as I beheld the huge blue and white Monash University welcome sign.

The campus was impressive with how everything was so clearly marked out with blue and white signs – even the car park had prominent white lines and labeling telling visitors where to park if it were small cars, big cars, disabled parking, and parking for pregnant women with prams.

As I took the footpath to the main building that was neatly lined with bushes and plants handpicked for just that spot, I dreamt of becoming and achieving something that my parents would be proud of. I was going to be the first in the family to attend a university, so it was a big deal.

I had orientation in the main building itself with its beautiful modern stacks of hexagon stories.

Big sliding doors opened to the main building to let me in.

It all looked very appealing and how it should look on my first day. I was nervous as I approached the Arts/Media center. I looked around frantically to find the reception area and walked towards it.

A tall, lean lady sat on what looked like a high stool, smiled as I approached her and asked me, "are you here for the orientation day today"? I shook my head with a small sigh of relief and followed her into a room where I stood timidly for a photo. It was for my student I.D. It was quick and easy, and I did nothing except smile a little and try to look orderly.

To my right was the enrollment office and to my left was the university café. Straight ahead was the long hallway to the library. The ceilings were tremendously high.

Outside stretched a big lawn near the library where it had little benches and tables and a quiet corner for study. There were a number of luxurious, peaceful spaces throughout the campus.

In the middle of the campus was a big lounge with relaxing sofas and a bar area for University parties. There were often theme parties that usually occurred late evenings on a weekday. Adjacent to that were outdoor barbecues with benches and wide vacant grassy areas.

At the other end of the campus were the student dormitories with fresh lawns surrounded by water fountains.

I browsed through the university lecture halls and then took the time to sit for a moment just to appreciate how lucky I was for this prophesied opportunity.

After a few minutes, the nice lady gave me an induction on how my oriented day would look on campus. She pointed out where the snacks lay and the direction of the library.

She handed me an intense information pack with the university campus map. Before she sent me off; she added, "orientation would be conducted in the main building itself with its beautiful modern stacks of hexagon stories. Don't get too lost and if you need help again, just pop by right here again". "Thank You, I will try not to get lost", I said, acknowledging her previous comment and made a swift turn to the direction I was meant to be walking in.

The other building across from where I stood had tiles that formed a geometric black and white pattern over its entirety. Each building has a different modern style inside as well as out. It all looked magnificent.

I spotted a nice vacant wooden bench near the library to sit down and just unload my belongings as I waited for the others to arrive.

I think I looked quite casual and tried not to make it obvious as my nerves got the better of me.

Just then, a girl who was about the same height as me approached me, stretched out her hand and introduced herself. From her accent, I gathered she would be from a similar country to mine. Before I made any assumptions, she boldly claimed she was from Bangladesh and had come here to study for a Bachelor's degree in Tourism and Accountancy.

As I got to know her, she made me feel like my normal self again. We comfortably walked around and talked a little before I met the other international and domestic students who were all studying different courses on the same campus.

My day passed by quickly, and my memory had rapid flashes of corridors, laughter, endless conversations, brochures, mini lecturers, subject browsing and just simple fulfillment.....

Suddenly.....It all went BLANK...BLURRRRR

I heard a SCREECHHHHHH..........BANGGGG..... There were ambulance sirens all around........

WHAT JUST HAPPENED!!!

I felt dead, I knew I was dead, I had to be.......there was numbness all over, and I felt like everything came to a standstill as I literally only had a heartbeat left.

Chapter 2

Number 33

The righteous cry out, and the Lord hears them;
He delivers them from all their troubles.
The Lord is close to the brokenhearted
and saves those who are crushed in spirit. —Psalm 34:17

"I hear my blouse ripping. I am startled and can barely see to the vantage of an observer hovering above my sprawling body!!......

Did it only come down to 14 days of being in this country after attending the most important day on campus. When tragedy struck!

Did God not want me to enjoy my second day of Orientation?. Did He not want me to pursue my education?

Was this his plan? How could it be? I am Dead! For GOODNESS SAKES SOMEONE WAKE ME UP!!"

There it was; I was declared BRAIN DEAD at the scene...

"Stand back; this has now become a crime scene", said one of the police officers, as the ambulance carried out my perished body.

It had come down to only 14 days in being in this country after attending the most important day at that point in my life, orientation on campus, not even one full complete day of university when tragedy struck.

Who would have ever thought just walking back from an ecstatic first day was going to be my ecstatic last day.

Who would have ever thought or those who knew me that this disastrous accident could leave me impaired physically and mentally, permanently.

I had innocently made a stop on the way back and had walked out of the convenience store, or milk bar as they call it, with a bag of too-good-to-resist snacks and the next thing I knew, my lifeless body was under the car.

This vicious car traveling at 80 km per hour had a student just like myself who subconsciously fell asleep behind the wheel and unknowingly was going to turn my life upside down.

Given all the injuries I had sustained and with no hope of recovery, my frantic parents, who so desperately took every possible course of action for either of them to get on the next flight to Melbourne, arrived in 4 days.

Lying there in the ICU with my almost shattered skull, a punctured lung and fractured pelvis, not knowing if the Lord would make an appearance yet. I just lay there brain dead with an 8% survival rate.

17th February 2007, 7:45PM

My distraught father made his way to the Alfred Hospital at a little past visiting hours. But due to the unfortunate circumstance I was in, he was allowed to visit me on the day of arrival. Before he arrived, he envisioned a white chair beside my hospital bed and yes, the white chair was still very much there when he arrived.

The symbolism of the white chair is from a religious aspect. It was very much associated with Jesus and the fact that he was all along near me and had never left my side. Obviously, all of the religious sides of things had no meaning to most people who were around me or who witnessed my accident, but it only made sense to a few who understood this miraculous event.

They say good things happen in threes. Three is the magical number in Christianity and theologically means the Trinity.

The trinity is the Father, Son, and the Holy Ghost. Three of these, and each have a meaning.

Just to give you a bit of an insight on Christianity, all Christians believe in the doctrine of the trinity. So what is the trinity? It is our God who eternally exists as the Father, Son and the Holy Spirit.

The *Bible* clearly discusses this doctrine in both the Old and New Testaments and Christians everywhere have always believed it. Someone has said it this way: If you try to explain the Trinity, you will lose your mind. But if you deny it, you will lose your soul.

I chose to have 33 chapters in this book; the most logical reason behind it is because 33 is the age of Our Lord when he died on the cross. Let's repeat this again - The age of our Lord Jesus Christ when he was crucified on the cross for our sins. Also, the number 33 is the numerical equivalent of AMEN: 1+13+5+14=33. AMEN is derived from the Hebrew AMEN, which means certainty, truth and verily.

Elohim, the divine name of God, is also mentioned 33 times in the story of creation in the book of Genesis.

That justifies 33 being a powerful and meaningful number.

Adam and Eve had 33 sons. The 33rd person in Jesus' lineage from Adam is King David, who ruled over the city of Jerusalem for 33 years. The Star of David is numerically represented as the number 33.

As you read this book, note how many times the number 3 appears (3 pm mass) or numbers divisible by three, such as nine – the number of days I was in a coma.

This book, of 33 chapters to honor Christ, deals with a prophecy. **Ezekiel 33:33** also concerns a prophecy: *And when this cometh to pass, (lo, it will come,) then shall they know that a prophet hath been among them.*

The power of the number 33 does not stop with biblical references. There are 33 complete turns in a sequence of human DNA and 33 vertebrae in the normal human spine. The modern Russian alphabet consists of 33 letters. Georgian is presently written in a 33-letter alphabet.

Chapter 3

Supernatural

"My right lung punctured.....

My lifeless body lay under the vehicle, and its driver passed out. The car, a white sedan with black rims, had come to a stop and hit me before anything else. The driver behind the wheel fell asleep, literally, behind the wheel. His fatigue caused my accident."

What's a Miracle?

Most days are the same. One after the next, with very few changes. You wake up in the morning, wash, have something to eat, and go about your business. Eat. Go about more business. Eat again. If you're lucky, you fit in some leisure time activity before going to sleep and repeating the whole cycle again. Every day. Day after day. With weekends varying slightly - if you're lucky.

Once or twice a year, you might get a little vacation that brings the variety of a few days at the beach or in the mountains or maybe in another country. Then it's right back to the same old routine.

Until…

A miracle happens.

What causes a miracle? Ultimately, you decide. For some, it is an experience that only the individual involved experiences. For some, only a witness can explain the unexplainable. Still, at the end of the day, it is an event that awakens your curiosity and becomes awestruck.

The most famous miracles are found in both the old and new testaments. Many Christians are familiar with the miraculous biblical stories, such as the partition of the Red Sea, in the old testament and Jesus Christ's resurrection from the dead found in the new testament. Some stories in the Bible may be dramatic while others are not so rushed and attributed to divine intervention, so coming to a conclusive elucidation, it has the same element, which is completely trusting in God.

For those who believe, truly believe, experience the unexplainable. Christ comes among us in many ways. For some, he has come in the form of visions. For others, he comes through prayer and for me, it was a personal encounter with my Lord, who had never left my side.

My parents, being staunch Catholics, never gave up on me or the situation I was in. Together they believed in the notion that 'God was going to work through me' and reveal himself through me. This manifested 'Trust in the Lord'.

It is stated in the beliefs and practices of Roman Catholicism that *'the plan of God, which is realized in history, is mysterious. It insisted that the existence of God's order is attainable to reason, and some of the fathers of the council wished to state that these truths were imposed upon reason by the evidence, a step that the council did not choose to take. Mystery does not mean the incomprehensible or the unintelligible. It means, in popular language, that humankind cannot know who God is or what God is doing or why God is doing it unless God reveals it.'*

A Catholic priest from the Divine Retreat Center in Muringoor, Kerala, came with a vision and his interpretation of the vision was "to go and study in Australia". My parents prayerfully examined the word of God and considered sending me across the globe to pursue my education.

Hence my reason and purpose for coming here, as in Melbourne, was to begin my career.

So as to say the horrific accident that left me brain dead where my brain dropped down to a level 3, which meant the blow to my head caused by a traumatic accident caused an impact known as the primary injury, leading to a traumatic brain injury (TBI).

Understanding TBI

A score that ranges from 3 to 15 helps the doctors classify an injury as mild, moderate, or severe. Mild TBI has a score of 13-15. Moderate TBI has a score of 9-12, and severe TBI has a score of 8 and below.

The impact of my accident caused my brain to crash back and forth inside my skull, which caused bruising, bleeding and tearing of my nerve fibers, and if I regained consciousness, then it was most likely I would not recognize familiar faces, would have had a blurry vision or my condition would either be stagnant or decline rapidly. So in accordance with this, the medical professionals claimed there was no hope because my brain had undergone a delayed trauma, which then caused it to swell where it pushed itself against the skull, reducing the flow of oxygen and causing a secondary injury. Therefore, both head injuries combined caused me to have TBI (Traumatic Brain Injury).

Another injury I sustained was a fractured pelvis. There was damage that occurred to the structural integrity of my pelvic region. This pain is aggravated by moving the hip or attempting to walk, but at this stage, I couldn't do either.

In addition to the fractured pelvis, I also had a punctured lung; primarily, a punctured lung occurs when air gathers in the space between the tissue lining, which causes pressure and keeps them from extension. There is a medical term for this injury known as pneumothorax.

I had several facial scars and abrasion scratches; there were bruises and lacerations that replaced my normal skin. It can sometimes take up to 12 to 18 months after an injury for a scar to heal.

From then on, there were medical surgeries suggested to keep me alive, but God knew I did not require any of it, and only He knew His purpose for this tragedy.

So some may call it a coincidence of events. Others may try to dismiss it as science. However you see it, all I know is that the doctors at Alfred Hospital could not explain my unexpected recovery in only 9 days after being hit by a white sedan traveling at 80 km per hour on the first day of my university orientation.

Who knew what would unfold.

The doctors not only pronounced me brain dead with little to no hope of recovery but instead asked my family to prepare my eulogy and to say their final goodbyes.

"If by some miracle she recovers, she won't recognize your face. She won't speak or walk for at least 6 months unless there is a miracle for her to speak sooner the medical team were heard saying" These are the usual predictions for a count level 3 of a Traumatic Brain Injury.

How could the impossible be made possible?

I say, through the power of prayer. Through the power of Jesus Christ!

Isaiah 53:5, "But He was wounded for our transgressions, He was bruised for our iniquities; The chastisement for our peace was upon Him, And by His stripes, we are healed."

Chapter 4

Anglo-Indian

"All the ends of the earth shall remember and turn to the Lord, and all the families of the nations shall worship before you." —Psalm 22:27

"My parents put their faith in the Lord, their underlying faith in Christ and His power to heal me in 9 days was simply MIRACULOUS!

And this only reason is why I get to share my experience and tell my story".

Authenticity

"I really want to be someone" was what I thought, "My Lord can do anything" is what I said and then realizing that it takes two to tango, which is God's help and your own strength to achieve something in life.

Growing up in an Anglo-Indian family certainly had its advantages; one of them is that our first language is English. Anglo-Indians are a distinct minority community in India.

Beginning in the 17th century, the British began to invade India. This led to Dutch and Portuguese settlers being encouraged to marry native women. These settlers, who were also employees, were promised a sum of money for every cross-cultural child born by the British East India company. By the 19th century, more British women arrived, and there were more mixed marriages and cultural offsprings.

The British East India Company built Fort St. George on the east coast of India, the Coromandel Coast. Named after the legendary 'soldier of Christ', slayer of dragons, venerated as the patron saint of soldiers since the time of the Crusades, the fort was built upon approximately two square miles (5 square kilometers) of Mandarze, a fishing village now called Channaipattinam. This little fort eventually grew into a city of about 66 square miles (170 square kilometers) that has a population of more than 7 million people. It is the fourth-largest city in modern India.

The British continued to expand their territory until they took over the majority of the subcontinent of India. From 1858 to 1947, The British Raj, also called the Crown rule in India, ruled the country for the British Crown. This area was commonly known as the Indian Empire.

The British brought many men from England to administer on behalf of the crown. The children of these men and local Indian women were often called half-caste. This process of British men blended with the native population of women also created the Anglo-Indian people in India.

When the term 'Anglo-Indian' was first used, it included all British people who lived in India. Which meant those of mixed British and Indian descent, precisely coming from a male line of Brits, were considered "Eurasians".

Thus, the term Anglo-Indian was used to indicate persons of mixed ethnicity.

The Government of India Act of 1935 proclaimed "a person whose father or any of whose other male progenitors in the male line is or was of European descent but who is a native of India" to be Anglo-Indian. And in 1950, India's constitution listed Anglo-Indians as an official minority group.

In addition to being of British descent and speaking English as our first language, the Anglo-Indians are of the Christian religious faith, which distinguishes us from other Indian ethnic groups, 79.8% of which (according to the 2011 census) practice Hinduism, 14.2% follow the teachings of Islam, 1.7% are Sikhs, and about 2% of the population are Buddhists. Only 2.3% of Indians are of the Christian faith.

Hence leaving my family and me under the 2.3% mark of Christians left practicing Catholicism.

Finally, when India attained its freedom from the British in 1947, it also left behind a westernized mixed ethnicity.

Thus, this is how Anglo-Indians originated.

Both my parents are Anglo-Indian and were raised in Calcutta. My grandmother from my father's side was partly German, and my great grandfather from my mother's side was a blue-eyed British.

My siblings and I all look very much Anglo-Indian, born with fair skin minus the blue eyes. Our appearances are very mixed; my brother and sister have lighter hair, as in a brownish tint, while I have darker hair.

Though both my siblings and myself have moved to the United States of America and Australia, we have not left behind our "Indianness". To elaborate, I mean our courteous mannerisms, our hospitality, our religious being and our gratitude…. from the land we come from.

Our culture highlights respect and kindness for the majority of us. Respect is extended across many dialects, in most ethnic groups and most prominently to our elders.

Respect is a significant aspect of Indian culture. It is also shown to people who are not related to you.

Chapter 5

Establishing the Family

Keep your lives free from the love of money and be content with what you have, because God has said, "Never will I leave you; never will I forsake you." So we say with confidence, "The Lord is my helper; I will not be afraid. What can mere mortals do to me?"
— Hebrews 13:5

"I had a fractured pelvis, my face and limbs bruised...

As I feel less overwhelmed, my fear softens and begins to subside. I feel a flicker of hope, then a rolling wave of fiery rage. My body continues to shake and tremble in slow motion. It is alternately icy cold and feverishly hot."

Luck or Blessed

What does my name mean?

Colette – People of victory or victorious people

Samantha – God has heard

Faustina - Lucky

All three names have true meaning, Victory, God is for me, and Lucky equivalent to Blessed!

It seems appropriate that my third confirmation name means "lucky" because my father considered me a lucky child since, as soon as I was born, his business flourished. He always told me ever since then that he wanted me to be physically present when he inaugurated a new business as I came with LUCK.

Personally, you create your own luck, and my luck comes from above.

My step-grandfather, who nicknamed me 'Colu', also considered me very lucky too.

In fact, he said the day wasn't perfect unless he remembered to call out to me before he left for work or to run errands, which was usually in the mornings.

"Colu", he would call, short for Colette, everyday between 8am to 9am. It was him who gave me my second name, Samantha, and since then, I have been officially "Colette Samantha Dixon". Faustina came later with my confirmation.

"Colu, Colu, Coluuuu come down and grab your chocolate", he would say. I would have usually woken up from my sleep by then and run down to greet him, or if I were still asleep, then my mother would send down the servant/maid to collect the item off him.

My father came from a middle-classed family, or I could say a mediocre family, where both parents worked.

My father, Clayton Dixon, didn't get the opportunity to complete his education. As he had to start early in life, by early, I mean, he had to earn a living and bring in an income.

Being the eldest in the family and my grandfather passing away of a heart attack when my father was only 19 forced him to grow up very quickly. The other siblings looked up to him for comfort and moral direction, and to support them, he worked on cargo ships where he would get a break to return home every three to four months.

In his early 20s, my father met my mother.

My mother, Carol Dixon, came from a very poor family and spent most of her days in a boarding school as her parents couldn't care for her and her brother, Burton.

Having lived in the somewhat quiet environment of a girl's hostel, my mother became a bookworm to entertain herself. She decided to quit school before she completed her education so she could earn a living.

To support herself, she worked as a typist for an electrical service organization from 9am to 5pm.

She was a simple and pious woman, also the eldest of her family. My mother had three younger siblings that she saw only once a year when she visited home from boarding school. She was used to it; she'd lived in boarding school since the age of three.

Both my parents were aspirational Catholics who believed in the Holy Trinity. Both were baptized as Catholics and raised as traditional Catholics. When they were 24, my parents tied the knot on June 7, 1986. It was the smallest wedding ever, of around ten people, including the priest.

My mother wore a wedding dress my father purchased while he was on tour/work on a ship in Singapore. Sadly, they couldn't even afford a wedding cake.

Though my parents were not strongly religious, they intended to raise us, their children, within the church.

They lived in a one-bedroom, one-room apartment, and my father was still working on the ships. A year after I was born, we moved into a bigger apartment in the same building complex, and then my father began experimenting with a few businesses with his 'lucky child' at his side.

Some were complete failures. Others were more successful. And finally, one was a complete success.

My father has owned this business for over 20 years. He hired chefs who cooked authentic Indian cuisine and a mix of Indo-Chinese Cuisine. And taaa…daaa it worked!

It was, in those days, traditionally unheard of for Anglo-Indians to establish businesses. They were looked down on by the other Indians in the community and did not associate themselves with the Anglos. It was probably because they thought Anglos couldn't and wouldn't make it, or they did not possess a trained mindset.

Generally, Anglos lacked funds for such endeavors or were preoccupied and afflicted with the not-so-business side of things.

Hence, my father chose an Indian rather than Anglo-Indian name for his restaurant –'Sher-e-Punjab'.

He started up his take-away food shop in May 1996 and slowly expanded it into a restaurant and additional takeaway shops. At first, he served excellent Indian cuisine that kept his clientele coming back for more. It was so good that they did not mind the Anglo-Indian owner behind the food that tasted so delicious. In this way, he made close contacts and connections with richer Indians who ordered on a regular basis allowing my father to establish a name for himself in Calcutta.

Though we lived in a modest neighborhood, my father was able to fund my education and take us on extravagant family holidays to luxurious hotel resorts.

Every couple of years, we would go on family holidays to Bangkok, Singapore, Malaysia, London, New York, or even short trips to towns around India to visit our extended family.

As a family, we would spend roughly a week or maybe a bit longer overseas, mostly in Bangkok, Thailand, or sometimes even Singapore.

In particular, I loved visiting Bangkok because of its exquisite Thai cuisine. I could not, and still cannot, eat any type of food without an enormous amount of spice like fresh chilies and sometimes even opt for the hottest chilies. Excluding breakfast and dessert, that is.

Bangkok is a truly magical city. My family indulged in everything the city had to offer. There were stunning tourist spots and street food, all worth exploring. As a family, we would scour the streets and take advantage of every delicacy. We stayed in sumptuous hotels with massive swimming pools and morning breakfast buffets. We enjoyed every moment!

My sister, Charisma, was a little too young to remember our holidays, but Calvin and I would walk down the busy Thai streets in the evening and sometimes even past midnight and either shop or eat while our parents were in their hotel room fast asleep.

We usually stayed in two separate rooms – my parents and Charisma in one and Calvin and I in another. That way, we didn't need to look after a younger child who was also our sibling. I think we were past that at that age or maybe too self-absorbed.

And Charisma got to stay with my mother, to whom she was still attached. Because of this arrangement, our parents often didn't know when we left our room. Or when we returned. And I can reminisce every second of it.

The last time we visited Bangkok and Pattaya, Thailand, as a family was when I had just turned 16. Since then, I went back with only my father for a couple of days when I had a layover in Bangkok on my way to India for a holiday from Australia when I had turned 21. I decided to do a little birthday and Christmas shopping for myself.

Singapore wasn't too bad, but the food wasn't up to my standards as my pallet only fancied spicy foods, and Singaporean food lacked it. The only thing I remembered in Singapore, apart from long walks on quiet streets, was the huge McDonald's they had on every corner. We wholeheartedly enjoyed McDonald's meals because Calcutta back then didn't have any yet.

My father would take us places to explore, like theme parks, snorkeling on beaches, ferry rides across islands, highly populated tourist destinations etc.

We even visited Sentosa Island, which was a huge part of Singapore. Initially, we had to catch a ferry to get there and a small tour bus to get around the island. Once, we even got lost and ended up in the same spot where we left. It took us an hour to walk to an adventure spot and back, and we had walked in a circle without realizing it. We'd definitely Laughed out loud!

One incident I particularly remember on Sentosa Island was the cable car ride in the theme park that was higher than others that I had been on. All five of us were allowed in the same car. I felt anxious and nauseous by the height of it as it moved along at a snail's pace. My father laughed and mucked around, shaking it deliberately, purposely trying to scare us. It took us 25 minutes to get to the other side, by which time I had grown quite sick.

We did make memories, and we lived to capture the great moments of our youth. We did strive to live our lives to the fullest. Till today I reminisce on those memories we created and cherish them with all my being.

Honestly and gratefully, we had a privileged life that had my siblings and me worshiping my father. It included household servants, maids, cooks, and chauffeurs, which was a very common thing in India.

I particularly adored my parents and I took their advice on literally everything. I remember having a lavish childhood in which my parents gave us the best of the best. Traveling around the world, the best education, tutors to excel academically, trying different cuisines at exquisite restaurants weekly! Pocket money that was more than we asked for! Apart from our opulent standard of living, we were disciplined. Disciplined beyond what one can imagine. Technically, I was the only sibling that was actually disciplined!

Chapter 6

The First Miracle

And behold, some people brought to him a paralytic, lying on the bed. And when Jesus saw their faith, he said to the paralytic, "Take heart my son: your sins are forgiven" —Matthew 9:2

"As I lay unconscious on the cold ground! Paramedics cautiously strap me down and take me to the farthest hospital, as my injuries sustained were beyond repair!"

Our first ever Family's First Miracle was attributed to my brother Calvin

Calvin – means and comes down from ancient Sumerian, which means "highly esteemed or valued". And my brother Calvin is.

George- Derived from the Greek word *georgos* and means 'farmer' or 'earthworker', which has a deeper meaning of having a prosperous future.

Born on the 12 of June 1989, Calvin is two and a half years younger than me. He wasn't expected to live past the age of ten. My mother and father were frantic when Calvin had to be rushed to the emergency room for an appendectomy at the tender age of just three years old. But that wasn't the worst of the news. After the surgery, he was diagnosed with Hepatitis B, a disease the doctors told my parents was incurable.

Hepatitis B is a disease that affects the liver. The infection can be chronic, meaning it can last for more than six months, and there is a risk of developing liver failure, which can lead to liver cancer and ultimately scars the liver. In short, there is no cure!

Hepatitis B virus is spread through body fluids of an infected person and needle-sharing.

When the virus enters the body, it attacks the liver cells and causes these liver cells to be damaged. In this case, patients with chronic hepatitis B are treated with medications like Interferon injections and Lamivudine oral medication to reduce the activity of the virus and prevent liver failure.

The most common symptoms are yellowing of skin and eyes, abdominal pain, especially in the area of the liver, loss of appetite, vomiting, fever, and dark urine.

So from then on, he suffered from a fever nearly every day as his liver was on the verge of failure. My mother had to watch in agony as a medical paramedic gave her son liquid injections in his tiny tummy every other day for 21 days every other month until he was almost seven years old.

But they saw only minor progress. Entrofro was given too. It was meant to reduce the activity of the virus in his system and prevent liver failure.

In desperation, my parents consulted different and the best doctors around the country. But it was the same diagnosis from all of them – my brother was highly unlikely to live to be any older and may not see his teenage years.

It was no secret in our building that my brother was ill. The neighbors saw the doctor's assistant who administered the shots come and go. They saw my parents' anguish.

They heard the whispers that he was not expected to live.

But the day arrived when a bold neighbor caught my mother in the hallway and said, "Do you know of the Miraculous center in the south of Kerala?" It is truly Miraculous and called the "Divine Retreat Center".

My mother's brows creased and she replied, "Can you please give me the details and I will speak to my husband and see if we can leave right away".

"Yes, sure", she said and continued to speak, "My cousin's best friend conceived after attending a retreat there." as she nodded her head vigorously. "There are others…those with disabilities who were healed after attending the retreat." Then she put her hand on my mother's arm, in the way of consolation, further saying, "Children who suffered from the last stage of cancer have also been healed completely."

Her voice dropped to a whisper. "It is so great. But it is only for those who have faith."

My mother contemplated the retreat. "It is a hope," she told my father. "Mustn't we try whatever we can?"

My father agreed, and away they set off to the miraculous land called Divine Retreat Center.

Chapter 7

Sanctuary of Our Lady of Vailankanni

And Mary said, "My soul magnifies the Lord, and my spirit rejoices in God my Savior, for he has looked on the humble estate of his servant. For behold, from now on all generations will call me blessed; for he who is mighty has done great things for me, and holy is his name. —Luke 1:46 - 49

"I felt invisible; every aching bone bled with sorrow through my anguish.

I don't know what changed.....I didn't know the difference between becoming a pioneer through tragedy or a slave to pity."

Spiritual

The Divine Retreat Center is located in the Indian state called Tamil Nadu, fairly close to the town of Vailankanni. In Vailankanni, there is a most special and sacred site. It is one of India's biggest Catholic pilgrimage centers. It is famously known as the Basilica of Our Lady of Good Health or as the Sanctuary of Our Lady of Vailankanni.

Why is it sacred to so many people? Three important miracles occurred at this site.

The First Miracle of Vailankanni:

Approximately 400 years ago, a huge banyan tree grew on the banks of a small pond near Vailankanni. Every day, a shepherd boy carried milk from Vailankanni ten kilometers to a rich man in Nagapattinam.

On one unusually hot summer day, the boy quenched his thirst with the cool pond water and was drawn to the shade of the banyan tree, where he leaned against the trunk to rest. Soon he fell into a deep slumber.

A vision of a Lady of celestial beauty appeared before him. She held a lovely child in her arms. The boy was spellbound by the heavenly vision of the Lady of unmatched beauty. She greeted him with a motherly smile and sweetly asked if he could spare some milk for her child.

Joyfully, the shepherd boy ladled up some milk for the heavenly baby. When a bewitching smile spread across the child's face, the boy felt a sense of deep satisfaction.

Later, when he delivered the milk to the rich man, he begged forgiveness for his delay and the shortage of milk. The rich man lifted the lid of the container. His brows shot up. "What shortage?" He asked for the pot was brimming over with milk.

In surprise, the boy related his experience to the rich man. He told him of the apparition he had had of the Lady of uncommon beauty and the cherubic child in her arms. The shepherd boy explained how he had poured out a portion of the milk from the container for the child at the beautiful Lady's request. He also mentioned how he had the unique pleasure of watching as the supernatural Lady fed the baby with the milk and the beatifique child's smile.

The master was fascinated by the extraordinary phenomenon the shepherd boy had witnessed and quickly made his way to the spot where the Lady and child had appeared. There, the rich man prostrated himself on the holy ground in great reverence to the Lady who had appeared to the milk boy.

The story of the apparition of the Lady and Child and the miraculous brimming over of the milk spread throughout Nagapattinam like wild fire. The Christians believed the Blessed Virgin Mary with the Baby Jesus had appeared in a vision to the shepherd boy. That they would choose such an unassuming place as Vailankanni to appear made their hearts overflow with great joy.

From that day forward, the pond became known as "Matha Kulam', Our Lady's Tank. Many travel there to be dipped in the holy water where miracles take place by applying it to diseased persons. A chapel stands now where Lady Mary appeared to the humble milk boy.

The Second Miracle of Vailankanni:

Around the close of the 16 th century, a poor widow lived in the village of Vailankanni with her congenitally lame son. In order to eke out a meager living, the boy sold butter milk in Nadu Thittu, a slightly elevated spot with a huge banyan tree with branches that reached out to provide shade for weary travelers.

Each day, the widow carried her lame son to Nadu Thittu where she left him to sell his buttermilk to anyone who took shelter under the tree. One extremely hot day, the boy waited for customers but no one turned up. He was disappointed because he and his widowed mother depended on the money of the travelers.

As with the milk boy a few years earlier, a Lady of stunning beauty suddenly appeared before him holding a dazzling baby in her arms. The Mother and Child wore impeccable white garments.

The Lady looked at the crippled boy with a charming smile and asked him if he could spare a cup of buttermilk for the cherubic child. The lame boy considered it a great honor to provide such hospitality to his ethereal visitors and quickly gave the Lady a cup of buttermilk.

With a sense of deep satisfaction, the boy watched the Lady feeding her child the buttermilk he had provided. The Lady bestowed a benevolent look upon the lame boy and turned towards her Divine Child as if entreating him to heal the cripple boy. Her silent request was answered, though the lame boy was unaware of the miracle wrought upon him.

The Lady thanked the youth for his generosity and asked for a favor. She begged him to go to Nagapattinam and relate the story of her appearance to a certain rich Catholic gentleman. Tell the man that the Lady wished to have a chapel built in her honor at Vailankanni.

"But I cannot," the boy protested. "I am lame and I cannot walk."

"Get up and walk. You are cripple no more," the Lady bade.

The boy leapt to his feet. His joy overflowed as he realized he could, indeed, walk. It wasn't enough. He ran as fast as he could, the whole ten kilometers to Nagapattinam. When he found the rich gentleman in Nagapattinam, the boy, once crippled, related to him the tale of the beautiful Lady and her beatific Child who had instructed him to build a chapel in her honor at Vailankanni.

The night before, the gentleman had also had a vision of Our Lady. In it, the Lady had requested him the same task, that he build a chapel in her honor. When the people of Vailankanni and Nagapattinam heard of the vision and saw the crippled boy's miraculous healing, their enthusiasm bubbled over and they all joined in to put up a small thatched chapel at Vailankanni just as the Lady requested. They erected an altar and a beautiful statue of Our Lady of Vailankanni with the baby Jesus held in her arms. This is the Shrine of Our Lady of Vailankanni.

Because of the many cures that take place to those who pray at the shrine, it has come to be known as Our Lady of Good Health Vailankanni (Vailankanni Arokia Matha). Recently, a chapel was erected where the Lady appeared and healed the lame buttermilk boy at Nadu Thiffu.

The Third Miracle of Vailankanni:

During the 16th century, European merchants established trading centers in India. The Portuguese had a special devotion to Our Blessed Mother Mary, and called her the "Star of the Sea". The Colombo, a 17th-century Portuguese merchant vessel, became caught in a terrible storm as it sailed west trying to reach the Bay of Bengal.

Violent waves assaulted the ship. The ocean smashed into it with a fury threatening the lives of all on board. The Portuguese sailors were devout Catholics. They instinctively fell to their knees and began to pray to Mother Mary to save their sinking souls. In desperate fervor, they prayed for rescue.

Suddenly, the sea calmed. Their prayers were heard as the winds quieted and the waves subsided. The ship soon safely made its way to the shores of Vailankanni. Immediately upon landing, the sailors vowed to build a church in honor of the Blessed Virgin Mary who had saved their lives when they had called on her in prayer. Immediately, they began to remodel the thatched chapel that had been constructed the century before by the rich man as Lady Mary had asked through the healed buttermilk boy.

From there emerged the Basilica of Our Lady of Good Health - the Sanctuary of Our Lady of Vailankanni.

Chapter 8

Calvin's Miracle

But the crowds learned about it and followed him. He welcomed them and spoke to them about the kingdom of God, and healed those who needed healing. — Luke 9:11

"There was no car collision and there was somebody to blame. The individual to blame slammed into the lamp post on the side of the road. As he drove right into it, his vehicle hit me. With the impact, I smashed his windshield and rolled under the car and became lifeless."

Pilgrimage

It was to this Vailankanni shrine that my family went in search of a miracle and then to the Retreat Center. Calvin, their beloved son and my brother, might not have lived.

Might they have another child? Might Calvin be healed? The Basilica of Our Lady of Good Health might provide another miracle – or even two – for my family.

But it's only if one believes.

Though we attended church every Sunday, like the usual Sunday-church goers, my parents lacked faith initially. And it had been four years that Calvin, my brother, had suffered. My parents attended the six-day retreat with my brother as a sort of last hope back in 1996. Not only for his healing but also in the hopes of my mother conceiving.

She had tried but had been unsuccessful. She was, after all, 35 years of age.

In those days, it was considered past the age when a woman should consider having another child.

It took a pilgrimage to reach the shrine beginning with the trip just to get there. From Calcutta, where we lived in the state of West Bengal (in the east of India), they journeyed by train for two days to get to the state of Kerala in the south of India, where the Retreat Center is located. It was only my parents and brother that went to attend the retreat; I was left behind with a couple of my maids.

They had to sleep on the train. The seats were converted into bed bunks to make it possible to lie down for the night.

So when they arrived at a station called Chalakudy, they took a taxi for about 20 to 25 minutes, which led them to the Divine Retreat Center in Muringoor.

Sometimes, but not always, we would visit the Shrine of Our Lady of Good Health because it too was in the south of India, though in Vailankanni, in the town of Nagapattinam district in the Indian state of Tamil Nadu. But my parents skipped the trip to Vailankanni this time and traveled directly to the retreat center instead.

We would usually kneel or walk the 1.5 km as a family. My mother would kneel every time we visited. Her knees were almost battered by the time she had finished because the surface was just sand covering concrete that, over the many years, had turned mostly to rubble. It tore up a pilgrim's knees very quickly. Yet, they, like my mother, showed their devotion to Mary, to the Lord, with their sacrifice/penance.

"Penance" also refers to acts that a believer imposes on him or herself outside of the sacramental context. Penitential activity is particularly common during the season of Lent and Holy Week (mainly the Passion week, inspired by Christ's suffering; hence in some cultural traditions still including flagellantism or even voluntary crucifix) and, to a lesser extent, Advent when penance is often combined with acts of self-discipline, such as fasting, voluntary celibacy, or other privations. In the Roman Catholic tradition especially, such acts of self-injury are sometimes called mortification of the flesh because of the belief that an unrestrained corporeal body endangers salvation unless controlled by the spirit, serving to detach the penitent of his worldly passions, as to draw him into closer union with God.[2]

Later, I would make this journey on my knees as well. Three times I crawled on my knees. When I was 19, right before the accident that forever changed my life, I made my first attempt to crawl; though I felt like I was to give up part way, my stamina took over. Then the second time around, I would succeed without the slightest hesitation.

Your eyes saw my unformed body; all the days ordained for me were written in your book before one of them came to be. Psalm 139:16

Chapter 9

The Divine Retreat Center

Strive to enter through the narrow gate, for many, I say to you, will seek to enter and will not be able. When once the Master of the house has risen up and shut the door, and you begin to stand outside and knock at the door, saying, 'Lord, Lord, open for us,' and He will answer and say to you, 'I do not know you, where you are from,' then you will begin to say, 'We ate and drank in Your presence, and You taught in our streets.' But He will say, 'I tell you I do not know you, where you are from. Depart from Me, all you workers of iniquity.' There will be weeping and gnashing of teeth, when you see Abraham and Isaac and Jacob and all the prophets in the kingdom of God, and yourselves thrust out. They will come from the east and the west, from the north and the south, and sit down in the kingdom of God. And indeed there are last who will be first, and there are first who will be last." —Luke 13:24 - 30

"There's something about trauma to the mind, body and soul. One day you're normal and the next, you're different; you don't know what changed, but you know nothing's the same and all of a sudden, you are learning to adapt yourself to the same environment with a whole new outlook".

The Inscription

You pass through the gates of the retreat center where a guard stands duty. Circle around a beautiful garden with a shrine to Mother Mary. Beyond that, you will come to the building itself, where you will see the above inscription. *"Come to me, all you who are weary and burdened, and I will give you rest. Take my yoke upon you and learn from me, for I am gentle and humble in heart, and you will find rest for your souls."*

—Matthew 11:28-30. These may be Jesus' most famous words.

The peaceful setting of the Divine Retreat Center is a Catholic spiritual place for the renewal of the people set on the banks of the river Chalakuday in Kerala.

The priests, who are also known as Fathers by the congregation, of the Vincentian Congregation's Mary Matha Province, with the blessing of the Catholic Archdiocese of Emakulam-Angamaly, have been 'graced by the Holy Spirit to be the open arms of the Lord to receive and convey the peace and healing of the Lord Jesus.'

My parents entered the Divine Retreat Center on Sunday and stayed until Friday, as that was the length of the retreat. No one could leave during the retreat unless there was a medical reason.

Retreats were held in the center in different languages, including English, so anyone could attend no matter their language. Food and accommodations were also provided for the price paid in advance. But there were parts of the center that offered free accommodation to those who could not afford to pay the price, food included for no charge as well.

The purpose of the retreat was to help the Christian faith become more alive in everyday life of contemporary people. The retreat would conduct a series of prayer exercises to deepen their conversion into a life with Christ.

The retreat, based on the Catholic sacramental and charismatic spirituality, is patterned over six days, where there is daily worship with the celebration of the Holy Eucharist, religious talks, sermons during mass, prayers with Eucharistic Adoration, the preaching of the word of God, proclamations of faith through testimonies and praise and worship.

Mostly, the retreats consist of prayer and worship. But in the evenings, the singing of hymns begins the healing sessions. These are often conducted by a priest or a minister who lives and works in the retreat center. The lights are dimmed so that people who are fervent in prayer or may have shed some tears cannot be seen. This helps them to avoid embarrassment as well as helps to focus attention on the altar.

Often, the priest or minister will begin to speak in tongues as he prays out loud while talking directly with the Lord our God. Not everyone has the opportunity to experience this, but only those who are very fervent in prayer. This deep experience of God will lead to the healing of mind, body, and soul. It will reconcile relationships as well as the past.

Returning to God is not an isolated event. It is surrounded by the path of healing in which the spirit is freed from addictions allowing the individual a channel of peace. Families are then able to reunite. The person thus healed can discover a mission and a purpose in life, causing them to radiate that healing they have received to everyone they encounter throughout the world. It is an empowering journey that allows them to go forth in their life with the mission of peace and love.

While the healing is in session, the priest will call out names of random people in the audience – those that suffer from an illness or a disability or perhaps are depressed.

The minister has not had the opportunity to meet these people as there are over 150 people in the crowd.

On the day, the priest said, "The Lord is telling me that there is a child here who is suffering from an incurable illness. Do not worry, says the Lord. You are being healed at this very moment. Jesus is covering you in his precious blood. Claim this healing, and you shall be healed."

My mother and father claimed this healing. My parents were drowned in prayer during the healing mass and they knew what they had heard during the healing proclamation was true. And they accepted it and believed with all the faith inside of them.

Jesus said, "Did I not tell you that if you believe, you will see the glory of God" —John 11:40.

When my parents and Calvin returned home from the Divine Retreat Center that year, they stopped my brother's injection treatments. Shortly after that, they took Calvin to visit the doctor. He confirmed that Calvin's liver was back to normal and there was no sign of the illness in the body – so he was healed!

But, of course, he should continue to return for regular check-ups. Which he did and his health remained excellent.

Divine Retreat Center is a miraculous Catholic retreat center, where I have seen miracles performed right before my eyes and my brother being a living miracle.

I have seen people experience an inner-self reflection through prayer in search of a deeper meaning in their lives.

I have seen others develop a contemplative stance to enable them to be present with the spirit within all things.

It is a place where people find liberating spiritual energy as a source of empowerment and some experience spirituality in a way that is self-soothing.

For my parents, it truly revitalized and rekindled their relationship with God. Both my parents sought a healing grace and attained a degree of spiritual healing.

It was this retreat center that enhanced their participation in Catholicism; it was this retreat center where my brother Calvin was healed of a severe life-threatening illness.

From then on, my parents were ecstatic. But a tiny part of their minds still questioned their faith and thought, "What if the illness is still there and his liver deteriorates over time? Or what if it came back?" That is when they decided that they would have another child.

My parent's devotion to the church increased. We began praying the rosary daily, along with saying other prayers. Every morning before school, my family and I would gather before the Holy Mother Mary statue that was sculptured against our wall in our house, to pray together in devotion. We would also repeat the entire verse from Psalm 91, where we recited it confidently from the top of our heads.

In January 1997, the Dixon family once again traveled to the Divine Retreat Center with the hopes that my mother might be able to conceive. My sister was then born on the 19th of September of that same year. Exactly nine months later.

Chapter 10

My Rebellion Side

"Due to all the injuries sustained, at this point, I required life support. My heart hadn't stabilized and my life depended on the machine.

Doctors mentioned that I would probably not survive with all my injuries.

There was swelling in my brain and I lay lifeless on the hospital bed transformed into a coma."

The Approval

Mostly, I was a good girl. By good, I mean I would always obey my parents, but sometimes their overbearing strictness caused me to be rebellious.

When did I have time to misbehave? The church was a part of my world. When we weren't saying the rosary, attending Sunday mass, or studying, I would either be on the phone with my best friend or thinking of the best excuses to attend a party on the weekend.

I was enrolled in a Catholic school called Loreto House; it is a private school that stood at the back of our church, and we attended on Sundays.

It was a massive white building. From the front, giant pillars on either side of the stairs supported the church spire, more than four stories in the air, topped by a sparkling white cross. Behind that, sprawling in three directions, three and four stories of the school perched over a basement level. It surrounded a basketball courtyard where we played each day.

I met my best friend Suzanne there. She was often my partner in crime and partner while I studied. Suzanne and I have made daring escapes from the school grounds and our houses and all those times were the best of my school days.

Mostly, I was well-behaved by my very strict parents and being the eldest, responsibility and pressure became overwhelming. They say oldest siblings are natural leaders and lead towards perfectionism. Back then, I did not know what it meant, but I saw myself as a wanna-be party girl.

My parents were not just strict but had high expectations and they may have taught me self-discipline.

It was my mother who made sure of that with her afternoon curfew and by waiting at the school gates in the family car driven by the chauffeur for the last bell to ring to pick me up. If I misbehaved, they punished me not only by spanking me with a belt – that was painful - but with emotional punishments too. They would send me to school with no pocket money or, far worse, with my hair oiled back with sticky coconut oil to embarrass me.

The other girls would laugh and point. And I would have to get through the whole day smelling like a coconut. Oh, how I came to resent that smell! There was no way to wash it out as oil repels water, so I would simply have to get through the day in utter embarrassment.

Suzanne and I experimented with different ways to convince our parents to allow us to have boyfriends. They were forbidden to both of us, though my parents were extreme. They wouldn't even discuss the topic of boyfriends. They didn't believe in a 'friendly relationship with the opposite sex' at that age; by that age, I mean 15-16 years old.

Did they honestly think boys would go unnoticed by us?

One day, we were trying to sneak out again. This time we were trying to escape a religious event. I was using the tried but repeatedly successful excuse of having a stomach ache. Only this time, my mother took it seriously. She thought I might have appendicitis because of my repeated complaints. I should have used a different excuse, but I fixated on this one because it had been so successful the last few times.

My mother was an expert at calling me out as a liar, but she hadn't yet detected this one. With the backing of our family doctor, my mother decided I needed to have my appendix removed immediately.

So on February 13th, 2003, ironically, the same date as I would have my future accident, I unwillingly agreed to have it taken out at the age of 16. I still bear a scar on my lower abdomen from the surgery. Sadly, I could no longer use that excuse. Surprisingly, my parents relaxed my rules slightly. I was allowed some daytime lunches after school, and shopping at the mall on occasion. But that's about it. I still couldn't be out after 5 pm.

I distinctly remember, when I was about 13 years old, it was a day in the 8th grade when I skipped an entire day of school to hang out with my mates. I left at 7:30 am, and this other classmate and I got a taxi and were driven into the city, where we ate fast food at a restaurant, drank milk shakes and strolled around without a care in the world. We did not do anything we were not supposed to, but I guess because from year 6 to about year 9, my parents justified their parenting style as it was beneficial, I felt I missed out on the nitty-gritty things teenagers my age did.

The day I skipped school, the whole time, I was thinking about how I would brag about it the next day to the other kids at school. Maybe even to my brother Calvin.

There were many of those who I had a crush on and vice versa but obviously couldn't date any publicly.

I have had several casual childish encounters but had never thought any more of it. Only because I had overprotective parents and I did not want to endure harsher punishments.

So after a day filled with fun and excitement (the excitement mostly from having broken the rules), we returned to the school just before the 2:20 pm bell pretending that we had been at the school the whole day – just like normal. My mother was there at the gates, leaning against the car, the chauffeur standing tall beside her. His face was blank, as always. But her mouth was tight. I knew that she knew. I had no idea that just five minutes after I left school, someone dobbed me in, saying I didn't show up. I never did find out who, or maybe I did and did not act on it as the deed was done.

My mother was furious. "How dare you skip school!" She growled once we were in the car and the doors were closed. Her face barely showed her anger. Anyone outside looking in would barely have noticed her disappointment. But the tone of her voice let me know that I was in enormous trouble.

By the time we got home, I was shaking in fear, trying to think of ways to escape punishment. She didn't have to tell me what she intended. I knew she would tell my father, who would then whip me. I had even written in my diary the night before, "If I get caught, I will surely get the belt." And I did. But this time, she ended up spanking me so hard that I could hardly stand to sit to eat dinner that night.

My comfort was feeding pieces of the food she'd cooked to my sister across the table, who pretended to be a dog while she completed her homework. Not laughing out loud! I had no desire to eat *her* food after she'd whipped me. So I rebelled again!

Usually after my evening tuition, homework and family dinners, I would lay on my bed and write my next rebellious act in my diary. What would it be? The tighter my parent's grip, the more I rebelled.

I think it was more of my frustration that led me to do things and get away with it. Distressed mostly, as I wanted to be treated like an ordinary teenager but never got to. My parents were the last of those sort of parents who would encourage their teenagers to go out and just 'hang' out.

I never did stand up to my parents, only because I was obedient and silently I knew they would always want the best for me.

Sometimes I would skip Spanish class. I took up an extra language outside school hours on a Wednesday in years 9 and 10. It was a two-hour class and I excelled in it. I did prefer to skip out at times, either early or miss it all together, to just do 'friend things.'

My parents were so strict that they wouldn't even let me go out for catch-up lunches and sleepovers were out of the question. So I had to do something. Somehow, I managed to ace all three Spanish exams every trimester in the end. Maybe because I self-taught myself too.

And all the time, I put up a front to my parents that I was a good kid who never did anything wrong. I had to because they threatened to hang me from the ceiling fan if I ever got pregnant or even had sex! Sex was to be saved until the sanctity of marriage. They said this even as they brought me up in strict Catholicism that preaches the sin of murder. It was a bit hypocritical and more of a hyperbole!

The hypocrisy extended to my brother. He was allowed to do pretty much anything. He was a boy, after all. In our Indian society or concept rather, boys hold a certain privilege. As they do over so much of the world. Girls have a certain reputation they must uphold. While boys are allowed to run wild, break the rules, and rebel without consequence. But my brother Calvin didn't skip school. He wasn't sneaky. He was just mischievous. He would pretend to study and draw instead. Or play video games to put off studying. Like one of those typical geeks!

He didn't need to rebel. He was allowed to go out after school in the evenings. He was allowed to stay out past 9 pm, even though he didn't until he was 14. After that, he was always out and away from the house. My parents were not strict with him. He was allowed to be out and party. But before he was 14, he was ordered to go everywhere with me…to my friends' birthday parties, to every after-school function, even to basketball matches I liked to watch – whether or not he cared about them.

And if I should speak to a boy, my brother would tattle – unless I bribed him with some of my precious pocket money.

Perhaps, though, it was all this adherence to rules that made it so imperative to me that I leave the country to attend school.

Suzanne and I were in school together up until year 10 at Loreto House.

Before I joined the Assembly of God's School which my father chose because he was an alumnus. He had spent his entire school life there. After my strict no-boys-allowed upbringing, I was surprised that my parents decided to allow me to attend my years of 11 and 12 at a coed school.

I made some friends there that I still remain in touch with to this day. Suzanne and I made different friends at our separate schools though we continued to have regular phone conversations. Due to our different exam schedules, though, we hardly ever caught up.

It was my dream that one day I would leave Calcutta, that I would leave India – and my family – to attend University in the United States of America. But that was not to be.

And we know that for those who love God all things work together for good, for those who are called according to his purpose.- Romans 8:28

Chapter 11

The Prophecy

And when this cometh to pass, (lo, it will come,) then shall they know that a prophet hath been among them.
—Ezekiel 33:33

"In the 120th hour, my distraught father arrived at the hospital. He watched as the doctor informed him of my deteriorating condition and that it would be very unlikely for me to recover anytime soon but a possibility of 6 months or I may progress into a vegetative stage".

"My eyes were still closed and I did not show any signs of awareness."

Doubting my Faith

I know I am not the only person who has doubted their faith. We have all been on this journey together – seeking to grasp our faith, to connect it with our practice. We all question and challenge our faith. Sometimes daily.

I imagine my soul as a cup longing to be filled with the Lord's presence. Yet, I realize that once this cup is filled, I may still thirst. For what do I thirst?

My mind said that I might as well assume that God exists as the church, as my parents tell me. Yet my heart remained dry and distant. It was precisely this emptiness, this incredible thirst, that kept me returning to His house to seek His presence every week.

Over time, while I was still a teenager, I began to realize that the voice of God spoke directly to my heart. I felt His loving arms wrapping around me and whispering to me,

"I am here." But I am forever dissatisfied with this infinite world, and it is that dissatisfaction that is a gift drawing me toward God Himself. It is every innate human desire, with its possibility of fulfillment that draws us towards the reunion with God that Jesus has promised each and every one of us.

Then we who are alive, who are left, will be caught up together with them in the clouds to meet the Lord in the air, and so we will always be with the Lord. **— 1 Thessalonians 4:17**

March 2004 – My 10th Year Exams

It was the year Mel Gibson's controversial film, *The Passion of Christ* was filmed. It was about the last 44 hours of Jesus of Nazareth's life. We were all eager to watch it. It was strategically launched in February, coordinating with Lent, the solemn Christian religious observance. According to the Gospels of Matthew, Mark, and Luke, it commemorates the 40 days Jesus spent fasting in the desert while he endured the temptations of Satan.

"Ma, this movie looks interesting. Can I please watch 'The Passion of the Christ'? And I promise I'll study after", I so desperately stated. "Yes, you may," replied my mother unexpectedly. "But make sure you go straight back to studying after; I do not want you to get a poor mark because we allowed you to watch a movie the day before your exam." "Yup," I nodded contently.

I was enduring my own temptations during this time as I studied for my ten-year exams, only taking breaks for sleeping and the bathroom. I even studied while I ate. These exams were crucial because of what they said to society. They were publicly posted on the internet for anyone to see. If I failed – everyone would know. There was no privacy at all because anyone could get online to view the results.

My parents were concerned that I might not pass because the year before, year 9, I had to resit a few subjects to move up to year 10 (subjects like math, Hindi-2nd language and home science/ economics). After I passed them, that is, the year 9 ones, some of my extended family members asked my mother about the exams. She never lied. Not even a little white lie, which can be annoying sometimes. The cousins poked fun at me, using every opportunity to rub it in, saying directly or indirectly that they were better in school than my brother and me. We usually ignored this only because we *lived* our childhood.

It was also difficult to 'just' avoid them because we all lived disgustingly close. Our apartment buildings were mere meters apart from each other or a few blocks down the road.

I know people who are insanely close to their cousins but speaking on behalf of my brother and me, we were never close to ours. It was just the usual family gatherings such as birthdays and occasional celebrations we would have to meet and exchange gifts. We never had any cousins from my mother's side, as most of them were from my father's side.

Growing up, my only friend in need was my brother, Calvin, as we hardly spent time with any of our cousins. We all had different appearances and personalities that we couldn't shake off.

In the third decade of my life, I have formed connections with some of my second cousins; I never had the slightest inclination that they existed.

Coming back to my initial year 10 pre-exam event, my parents and I decided that I should take a break from my studies for the exams to watch "The Passion of Christ." It gave me a sense of awe and wonder about the spiritual world and the incessant emptiness and dryness that defined the depths of my internal life. It inspired me at the age of 16 to put mind over matter. If Christ is truly present in the Blessed Sacrament, it could change everything. The thought gave me the motivation to give the exam my best shot. I gave it my all and successfully passed my year 10 exams – all 11 subjects! Given my academic history, my parents honestly did not think I would succeed. They were thrilled.

It gave me a joyful beginning to year 11 a few months later, and the next two years flew by quickly. Before I knew it, I was back in the exam zone for my year 12 exams. I had thought year 10 was crucial. But my year 12 exams were more like a life or death scenario because of what my future held if I scored high enough. This exam was not just about passing – I needed a good score to get into a good university. Wherever I chose to go would require a *good* mark, not just passing marks.

So I found myself, sometimes for hours, in front of the tabernacle of the church, trying to act as I should in front of the supposed presence of Christ, still having trouble believing. I was riddled with questions and longing for wholehearted faith in God and heard myself say, "Lord please guide my path, anoint me with your Holy Spirit so that I can feel you working through me."

I felt I was falling short of any semblance of the genuine faith that had previously briefly prevailed when I'd seen 'The Passion of Christ'.

But I took the year 12 exams. I sat for English, geography, economics, home science, and elective English. The exam hall was a massive room on top of the building used as a sports stadium for big events. It was often rumored to be haunted, stories that were encouraged by the cleaners. Waiting for the supervisors who walked about for the duration of the exam to say, "You may begin," we students were gripped with fear. The exam would take two to three hours to complete.

Examinations in India are beyond frightening as it distresses the youth at an early stage in their life. Honestly, the examination itself is doable, but it is the intense academic pressure that accompanies it. It is the deliberate tortuous anxiety and that panic effect atmosphere that the individual holds on to, mostly lifelong.

The most common norm/s are depression and anxiety, with mental health disorders that top it off. But in comparison to the academic pressure here in Australia, there is hardly any pressure or no pressure (speaking from a teaching point of view). Students here try their hardest and succeed, making it practically possible to achieve an accomplishment and are in no way under insurmountable stress like 17-year-olds experience back in India.

Speaking of exams, Australian students of years 3, 5, 7 and 9 get handed the National Program for Literacy and Numeracy (NAPLAN) test under strict test conditions, a set of four or five tests that students sit over three days in Term 2 of the school year.

On an international scale, these tests are significantly lower than average compared in some countries.

But the Australian curriculum is designed so that all Australian children better understand their learning and potential. Moreover, in Australia, most of the evaluation of a student's academic improvement is assessed and not tested.

Thus, students undergo many assessments and the best of which is considered and graded. On the whole, they are devoid of any pressure to perform.

Whereas the Indian education system is based on theories before the concepts of being practical.

The 'D'day of my year 12 examinations arrived, and my entire body was numb. I was surprised that I could pick up my pen, which I chose carefully to be certain it would continue writing throughout the entire test. If it stopped writing and I had to replace it, I would lose valuable minutes of writing time.

When the exams ended, I bit my nails as I waited for the results to upload from the internet and appear on the computer screen. Yet again, anyone with my name and ID number could view the results, so it would be most embarrassing either way..

So, good news, I passed – with good scores – more than enough to get me through to the other side of the world.

I was ecstatic. And so were my parents. They rewarded me with a mobile phone on my birthday. It was one of the biggest things I had ever gotten and I was ever so grateful for it! What an excellent reward.

I immediately bought books with all the American universities listed in them. I lay on my bed in the afternoons flipping through it, reading the descriptions of each school.

Columbia University in New York, University of Pennsylvania in Philadelphia.

Goucher College in Maryland, the University of Michigan in Michigan, Colorado College in Colorado, UCLA California and Stanford. I looked at them all and marked off the ones I wanted to apply to. I was so excited at the thought of finally achieving my goal of going to the United States of America!

But yet again, God had another plan for me.

The Prophecy

The Divine Retreat Center played such a big role in our lives. When we attended the retreat, on this visit, a life-changing miracle was predicted.

"Sanctify me, oh Lord, Cleanse my body, mind and soul, purify me and make me whole." These were the words of the song that resonated with me after the first day's session at the retreat hall. As the session came to an end and most people had left to go outside the retreat hall for an interval, I looked up at the massive altar that lay in front of me, where the arms of Jesus were open and called upon any soul and mine was an anxious soul.

A message, particularly for me, was delivered through the head priest. The priest told me that he had prayed so that I would make the right decision on where to study. His words were distinctive and clear.

"God is going to work through you," he told me. "You must go to Australia. The U. S. is not the country for you. The Lord will work with you in Australia. It is there that you must go," he said firmly.

After hearing his prophecy, I returned home. Once again, I lay on my bed with a book listing all the universities – this time in Australia. Again, I read through all the descriptions of the many schools across a big country and chose the ones, reluctantly, that I could attend. I began applying to the best universities around Australia until I got accepted into Monash University in Melbourne.

Chapter 12

The Day of the Accident – First Day of University

To do whatever your hand and your plan had predestined to take place. —Acts 4:28

"On the 7th day of my accident, my father returned to the hospital, in blind faith that I would talk to him... soon... fairly soon. Doctors and nurses around the room looked upon my father and me anxiously."

The Brief Walk

It took me 9 minutes to walk back from the station to the milk bar when a white sedan plowed onto the wrong side of the highway and emerged onto the footpath. The vehicle ran over me at 80km/hr as it headed straight for the lamp post that was located on the median strip.

Calcutta

Calcutta was officially changed to Kolkata in 2001, but I still like to call it Calcutta. Calcutta is situated in the West Bengal state and is one of India's largest cities and ports. It is also considered to be one of the overpopulated cities in India, and its dominant language is "Bengali." I do understand the language but cannot speak it as fluently as I can speak "Hindi." The city is well known for its art exhibitions and concerts.

Calcutta has its own beauty – the ancient ornate buildings, the beautiful colors everywhere. Calcutta is nothing if not colorful. The streets are crowded with people packed shoulder to shoulder, the noise of honking horns and voices, and animals, the smells of so many bodies, and vendors cooking, and exhaust. People pushing. People rushing. It was always chaotic.

Melbourne was a different world. Compared to the crowded streets of Calcutta, the streets of Melbourne were practically deserted.

As we all know, Mother Teresa, also known as the saint of Teresa of Calcutta, lived to serve the poor. She was a gentle soul who eased their suffering and helped them come out of extreme poverty. Mother Teresa traveled to India to become a nun, where she began her journey as a teacher, followed by becoming a principal. It was then that she received a spiritual calling and left the convent to start her own charities to care for the orphans, and the terminally ill and give the poor a place to stay.

Our great Mother Teresa from the Missionaries of Charity in Calcutta had been canonized as a saint on the 4th of September, 2016.

It was when Mother Teresa was recognized for her second miracle, a Brazilian man who suffered from brain tumors was healed after the family prayed to Mother Teresa for help.

Mother Teresa died on the 5th of September, 1997, at the age of 87.

I was one of those privileged citizens who got to attend a future saint's funeral in the city of Calcutta.

* * *

I had been driven or chauffeured everywhere I went for my whole life. I felt lost having to find my way around Melbourne, and that 'lost' feeling carried on to the day, 14 days later, when I made my way for the first time to Monash University via public transport on my own. Those first days, I spent getting myself oriented to Melbourne and settling in with my host family.

The people I lived with were a husband and wife – the husband, an atheist, and the wife, a firm Catholic believer, who also were known through family friends in Calcutta. They had no children of their own and would visit Calcutta often for holiday purposes. My parents paid them a monthly fee, as did other international students to whom they offered room and board.

In those first days I spent in Melbourne, they took me shopping in the malls and food markets and showed me around the beautiful new city.

Chapter 13

Friendships Built

And without faith it is impossible to please Him, for he who comes to God must believe that He is and that He is a rewarder of those who seek Him. —Hebrews 11:6

" I had an abrasion on my scalp, 1.5 cm laceration on my upper right side of my stomach and a laceration on my lower back. My pelvis needed to be repaired with an external fixator in the operation room."

Building Mutual Trust

That day, I made two friends, one was a sweet dark-haired girl from Albania and the other was a modern Buddhist girl from Bangladesh. Eliana was tall and thin with pale skin and a friendly personality. She wore very modern clothes with her nails perfectly painted and sprayed up hair with a minimum amount of makeup.

We also met Devi, who came from Bangladesh with a full scholarship. She was small and cute with a somewhat Asian appearance. She had almond-shaped eyes that sparkled with mischief and fun.

We went to get our University I. D. cards made up, including our photos attached.

I looked lost in mine and requested a second shot – which was refused. Pouting a bit, for I was used to getting my way most of the time, carelessly, I shoved it in my wallet. It was that university card that later allowed the police to identify my lifeless body.

On the day of my accident, my hosts were supposed to pick me up, but they were unable to due to work. So when I got ready to head back to the accommodation where I was living, which was roughly about 20 minutes away by train.

Eliana, the girl who offered me a ride home, had been living in Melbourne a few years by then and so was able to drive. The reason for my refusal was that I wasn't used to trusting anyone so soon that I didn't know *very* well or just met. I'd been chauffeured most of the time or driven by my parents, and my brother had accompanied me almost everywhere when my parents hadn't, so it seemed so strange to be out on my own at all.

To be in the car with a stranger just seemed too much.

So around 3:50 p.m., I headed back to my accomodation the same way I'd gotten to the University – by train.

It was about 4:20 when I arrived at my stop called Sandown Station. I had to think for a moment to refresh my memory as to which direction to turn.

Sandown Road was a broad, main road with driveways diverging off of it to the few homes along the fence.

But mostly, the land on the far side was vacant. I stopped into a milk bar on the other side to buy some snacks as I was ravenous despite the sandwich I'd eaten earlier.

As I stepped back outside from the convenience store, I opened the chocolate bar, scrunched its wrapper and began to eat it, headed towards where I would cross the road. I had only gone a few steps…..WHEN……at that moment, my world changed.

I couldn't remember all of it. It was hazy, vivid…

I just smelt the inkinesss of blood around me;

I gasped as I tried to fit parts of it together, my teeth screeched, I hated the sound of that metal hitting against me…..

Chapter 14

The Immediate Aftermath

For the LORD watches over the way of the righteous, but the way of the wicked leads to destruction. —Psalm 1:6

"There are major surgeries required" the doctor said to my father who stood there blankly as she checked my dressing on my hip and rechecked the probe that drilled a small quarter on the top of my head into my brain with a tube running off into another machine. The incision looks swollen and angry, puffing up around what seemed like hundreds of staples running across my sides. I had devices on my legs to prevent blood clots with tubes running to yet ANOTHER monitor..

13 February 2007

I, Colette Samantha Dixon, was identified from the University I.D. that I disliked and was airlifted to the Alfred Hospital. Luckily, they found my backpack with my phone as well. With my only I.D. being my University I.D., 'they simply dialed the first contact number on my phone – the letter A – to notify that lucky person. They called Andrea, the first contact on my phone, a family friend who had settled in Melbourne not long before I arrived.

It was so fortunate that Andrea was a family friend and not a stranger that I might have just met, only because she knew how to reach my family and she delivered the awful news. Andrea called my family back in India and gave them the terrible news of my horrific accident with as much detail as she knew. My parents had emotional as well as physical reactions when they heard the news of my accident.

It caused such physical and mental stress that my mother was barely able to function, to continue in her care of my other two siblings. My father had difficulty making the necessary arrangements for a visa and air travel to Australia, where I lay dying, according to the reports from the host family, who contacted them and gave them as much news as they could. They drove down to the hospital to be with me. They panicked when they found out that the doctors weren't sure if I would make it through the night.

"Why," my parents questioned God, "did you do this to our family? Have we not given you our devotion? Prayed to you every day? Attended your church and observed your holidays faithfully?" Tears flowed down the faces of my father, mother and siblings.

They were emotionally numb and all in a state of utter shock.

They felt helpless as their oldest child lay in an emergency room miles away on the other side of the world, as though the air had been sucked from their windpipes or they had been punched in the stomach. They could barely draw breath. My father immediately applied for an emergency visa – a tourist visa usually took two to four weeks to process, but an emergency visa is sooner. My mother would have to remain in India to care for my two younger siblings.

Fortunately, it only took three days for the visa application to be approved, and my father arrived in Melbourne on Saturday, February 17th.

Within 24 hours, everyone back home, in fact, most of Calcutta, knew about my tragic accident. Close friends and extended family were devastated. Aware of the horrific injuries I had sustained, no one thought I would make it through the week.

In Melbourne, the news spread across the University of Monash, where I was enrolled.

People and priests were on their knees repeating prayers for someone who was far away on another continent, fighting for my life. Masses were offered, and vigils held.

The girls I had met at the university on the day of orientation, Eliana and Devi, also found out about the tragedy from Glenda, our University chaplain.

Most of those who knew about my accident were surely praying for my recovery, yet knowing the hopelessness of the situation that even the qualified medical professionals had little hope for my survival, they prayed more for my family and how unfortunate it was that I'd met with such a horrific accident.

Rehashing the Accident Scene

Heading north on Princess Highway, the nineteen-year-old boy was tired after having put in a long day studying at Monash University. Yes, Monash. But not the same campus I attended. Still a teenager himself, who had just sat for a long exam and with no sufficient sleep the previous night, drifted to sleep, and his car swayed off the road and onto the footpath where I walked.

The sun was in his face, but that didn't keep him fully conscious as he drove into the pedestrian girl, me, while traveling at 80 km (appx. 50 miles) per hour.

His white sedan hit me before smashing into the lamppost on the corner.

Glass shattered. Tires squealed. Other cars slammed on their brakes. People jumped out of their cars to see if they could help. Or just to see. Whatever it was, I lay on the footpath in a sticky pool of blood. It gushed from my skull. There were screams, shivers and aghast expressions.

My entire body smashed against the car windshield; I had tumbled from its bonnet, and my battered body rolled head first to the ground. My heart raced and skipped a beat. My knees bent with the impact and my torso jolted backward. My excessively torn clothing was covered in red and black stains, and my neat suburban ponytail and my head were within the red sea.

There were fresh puddles of bloodshed just covered in the ground. There was also a thick layer of blood dripping through the sides of my head and between my ribs. There was a sense of loss; I felt a stiletto heel between me on either side; my eyes stared at the slanting sunlight stretched right across my strewn clothing as I could feel my skin being torn apart and the pain gushed through my bones like a thousand sharp blades. I felt my head being pushed vigorously into the end of a blunt nail. I felt impaled by the metal hooks on the car that grazed my flesh;

I reached forward with a wail of despair, but my hand grabbed the thin air. I couldn't breathe as I lay expressionless under the car when Elaina's voice resonated through my head like an echo……………………………………..

"Do you want a ride home?"

I whimpered, and I yelped before passing out.

A man grabbed his wife as she started to slump to the ground in a faint.

"Call an ambulance," he cried. Though he was pretty sure the girl on the pavement was past the need for medical help. His stomach began to clench. He had to look away before he...oh, God! He gasped!

Fire engines responded in case the car that hit the lamp post might burst into flames. Police cars zoomed to the scene. And ambulances arrived for the girl, me and...well, whoever might have fainted in response to the spectacle of all that blood.

Emergency responders in reflective vests hurried about the scene, some just to hold back bystanders. "Was he drunk?" Asked someone from the crowd as they assisted the driver from his car. "Was he on drugs?" asked the other. "I think he was sleep deprived," said the third. "Geez" exclaimed the other.

As these speculations were made, only God knew what was to become of me. It didn't take long before reporters arrived on the scene. They heard the question and jotted it in their notes. "Sleep Deprived student hits a teenager."

"Braindead," they heard an ambulance tech mutter. The sloppy reporter only jotted down 'dead,' and that's what came out in his newspaper in contrast to the 'live at the scene' reel being shot with an ambulance strategically blocking the blood-covered sidewalk. The next day, three newspapers claimed me dead: two at the scene, one in the emergency room.

The police cordoned off the area where I lay. If I were to die, they would need every scrap of evidence – every skid mark, every piece of glass, every drop of blood.

The day after next, more newspapers reported that I had tragically died on the day. One claimed I died after the man crashed into me, and the other said, "Braindead: Lost too soon."

Braindead is not *actually* dead. It left some hope. However, little.

Braindead determines that there is no life within, that in a couple of days, the brain will completely shut off and the organs will stop working. About 90% of patients who have been determined to be neurologically brain dead will either die or remain in a permanent vegetative state. However, this does give their loved ones time to say 'goodbye'.

It also means the damage to the brain is irreversible and the person would need a life support machine to keep their heart beating as they will never regain consciousness or breathe on their own.

I had suffered multiple and complex injuries and was given a 8.1% chance of survival.

"Her injuries include fractures to her rib cage, a fractured pelvis and internal injuries to her lungs and a pancreatic bleed. The injuries are extensive and her prognosis is initially shocking", exclaimed one doctor to another.

Chapter 15

Confirmation

If we confess our sins, he who is faithful and just will forgive us our sins and cleanse us from all unrighteousness. —1 John 1:9

"After a moderate to severe brain injury, swelling, bleeding or changes in brain chemistry often affect the function of healthy brain tissue. The injured person's eyes may remain closed, and the person may not show signs of awareness.

But, my father, Clayton, a man of extraordinary faith, truly believed in the Our Miraculous Savior Jesus Christ. He believed that God's angels look over us all. And that they were looking over me".

The Name

My confirmation name is Faustina. The Sacrament of Confirmation is the second of the three sacraments of the Christian initiation. To become a full member of the Catholic Church, one must receive the three Sacraments of Baptism, Confirmation, and the Sacrament of the Holy Eucharist (Communion).

Baptism

A person must receive The Sacrament of Baptism to wash them free of the original sin with which they were born. It is often called 'the door of the church' since most Catholics receive baptism as infants and are, thus, entered into the life of the church.

The Sacrament of Baptism is the beginning of life – supernatural life. According to Catholicism, we come into the world with a soul which is supernaturally dead. Baptism gives us supernatural life, the result of God's personal and intimate presence within us.

It is given to us in Baptism when we freely accept it in the sacrifice Jesus Christ made for us upon the Cross. We make that acceptance by receiving the Sacrament of Baptism. Original sin disappears and God is present in our souls as we are filled with the sanctifying grace.

First Holy Communion

Then a Catholic does a First Holy Communion, which they generally begin studying around first grade. Children who attend a Catholic school receive their religious instruction in classes there. Otherwise, they study after school or on the weekends in catechism. Generally, it takes about two years to study for this Sacrament.

First Holy Communion is considered one of the holiest and most important occasions in a Roman Catholic's life. It means the person has received the Sacrament of the Eucharist – the body and blood of Jesus Christ. Most Catholic children receive their First Holy Communion at the age of seven or eight, which is considered the age of reason. Others take their First Holy Communion whenever they have met the Church's requirements.

A person must be without sin, in a state of grace, in order to receive communion. Therefore, the Sacrament of Baptism must have been received, and confession must be made. Traditionally, children make their first confession, known as the Sacrament of Penance, the week before receiving their First Holy Communion. At their confession, which is given in a booth in which the parishioner is on one side with a screen dividing him from the priest on the other, the child details any sins or misdeeds they have committed to a priest to receive a penance. The penance is usually several prayers they must recite immediately upon leaving the confessional. This absolves the person of all sin, making them ready for communion.

By the laying on of hands and the anointing with Chrism Oil, which first happened at Baptism, Confirmation confirms the Catholic child with the fullness of the Holy Spirit, thus completing Baptism. 'Confirmation' reminds them of their participation in the ministry and mission of Jesus and strengthens them to follow Jesus more closely. This generally happens around the age of 13 or 14.

Consequently, I was confirmed and received the name "Faustina".

Chapter 16

Faustina

And He said to him, "'You shall love the Lord your God with all your heart, and with all your soul, and with all your mind.' —Matthew 22:37

"Towards the beginning of my heavenly adventure, I was surrounded by clouds. Big, puffy, blue-white ones. At a distance, white winged beings who shined with a soft wavering light paced through the sky- were there angels? "

Vegetative State

As I lay on the hospital bed still unconscious from the anesthetic as well as a coma and was incubated on a respirator to regulate my breathing, as it ran off into a machine, my lips were cracked, swollen around, my tongue dried out and my face was still bruised. The nurse felt sadness as she knew I was never bound to come around soon or even at all.

Thoughts of a vegetative state ran through her mind; another term for this is

Unresponsive Wakefulness Syndrome

It is where the patient can breathe on their own and their eyes are usually open. They sometimes have sleep-wake cycles and reflexes functioning, but they hate noise and though get startled by visual stimulation along with minimal movements, they cannot communicate.

Faustina

My third confirmation name is Faustina, named after Saint Maria Faustina Kowalska of the Blessed Sacrament.

Helena Kowalska was born on August 25, 1905, in Glogowiec, Leczyca County, in the northwest of Lódz in Poland. She was the third of ten children in a poor, religious family. At the age of five, she had dreams of 'walking hand in hand with the Mother of God in a beautiful garden.'

At the tender age of just seven years old, she first felt a calling to religious life when attending the Exposition of the Blessed Sacrament, when the Holy Eucharist is solemnly exposed to the faithful so they may pay their devotions. It was then that 'for the first time, I heard God's voice in my soul; that is, an invitation to a more perfect life.' Helena experienced a call to grace.

'After receiving her first sacraments of Confession and Holy Communion, Helen seemed most intent on praying. Her early rising and frequent and prolonged praying concerned her parents. Helena would respond that her guardian angel must have awakened her to pray. She went to weekly confession, and each time would beg her parents' forgiveness. Adhering to an old Polish custom, she would kiss her parents' hands before asking for their forgiveness. Her parents noted that they did not ask any of their children to do this and that none of their other children followed this practice.'

Because Russia occupied Poland at the time, Glogowiec was forced to close its schools during most of Helena's grade school years, meaning she only had two winters of schooling. She began her education as a 12-year-old second grader. But she was asked to leave during her third term, along with the other older students, to make room for the younger students. Besides, her help was needed on the farm at home to help tend to her younger siblings.

The family was so poor that they shared one dress among all three daughters. So that each daughter could wear a dress to mass on Sunday, they attended three different masses, exchanging the dress amongst them.

By the time Helen was 14, the two older sisters had left the family farm to become housemaids. Helen asked for permission to do the same and her parents granted it. Then she asked to enter a convent that required the donation of a dowry. But they were a poor family that could not afford such an offering. Helena temporarily gave up her ambition of joining the convent.

A short time later, she attended a dance with her sister Josephine when she experienced a vision of Jesus in suffering, asking her, "How long shall I put up with you and how long will you keep putting Me off?"

Helena left the dance to go to the Cathedral of St. Stanislaus Kostka, where she prostrated herself on the floor before the tabernacle to beg the Lord to direct her to His will. He answered, "Go at once to Warsaw; you will enter a convent there." With no belongings but the dress she already wore, she immediately set out for her destination, praying to the Mother of God for guidance. Along the way, she received guidance from the Lord, telling her what to do next. Messages such as, 'Go to that priest and tell him everything; he will tell you what to do next."

These messages started what would be 13 years of daily communications with God that included visions, ecstasies, bi-locations, prophecies, interior messages, and the knowledge of the condition of souls.

Faustina was thoroughly tested to prove her sanity. To show her messages were indeed from God, Faustina's mentor encouraged her to keep a diary. In it, Faustina wrote:

"In the evening, when I was in my cell, I became aware of the Lord Jesus clothed in a white garment. One hand was raised in blessing, and the other was touching the garment at the breast. From the opening of the garment at the breast, there came forth two large rays, one red and the other pale. In silence, I gazed intently at the Lord; my soul was overwhelmed with fear but also with great joy. After a while, Jesus said to me, 'paint an image according to the pattern you see, with the inscription: Jesus, I trust in You.'"

Faustina also described in that same message, Jesus explaining that he wanted the Divine Mercy image to be "solemnly blessed on the first Sunday after Easter; that Sunday is to be the Feast of Mercy."

Faustina, not knowing how to paint, asked around her convent for help but was denied. It wasn't until three years later, in 1934, that the first painting of the image was created by painter Eugene Kazimierowski.

At the age of 21 years, Faustina showed signs of illness and had to be sent now and again from the convent to rest as she was convalescent.

In 1932, Faustina returned to Warsaw, where, on May 1, 1933, she took her final vows to become a perpetual sister of Our Lady of Mercy.

Thereafter, on Good Friday of 1935, Jesus told Faustina that he wished for the Divine Mercy image painted by Kazimierowski to be publicly honored and seven days later, a priest delivered the first sermon on the Divine Mercy.

In her diary, Faustina also wrote about her vision of the Chaplet of Divine Mercy which is used to 'obtain mercy, trust in Christ's mercy and show mercy to others'.

The following year, Faustina tried to begin a new congregation for the Divine Mercy. She further writes, Jesus said to her, *"My Daughter, do whatever is within your power to spread devotion to My Divine Mercy. I will make up for what you lack."*

That same year, Faustina became ill again and was sent to the sanatorium in Pradnik, Krakow, where she spent most of her time in prayer.

Holy cards of the Divine Mercy image were created in 1937 with the Novena of Divine Mercy message providing instructions on them. It had been given to Faustina by Jesus.

The Novena is a tradition of devotional praying repeated for nine consecutive days or weeks (nine to honor the nine months Jesus spent in Mary's womb). The nine days when the disciples gather in the Upper Room devoting themselves to prayer between the Feast of the Ascension and nine days until I woke up from a coma.

Novenas are vital in the Catholic faith and are usually prayers of petitions but sometimes prayers of Thanksgiving.

The Divine Mercy Novena:

In the name of the Father, the Son, and of the Holy Spirit, Amen.

Today bring to Me ALL MANKIND, ESPECIALLY ALL SINNERS, and immerse them in the ocean of My mercy. In this way, *"you will console me in the bitter grief into which the loss of souls plunges Me."*

Most Merciful Jesus, whose very nature it is to have compassion on us and to forgive us, do not look upon our sins but upon our trust, which we place in Your infinite goodness. Receive us all into the abode of Your Most Compassionate Heart, and never let us escape from It. We beg this of You by Your love which unites You to the Father and the Holy Spirit.

Eternal Father, turn Your merciful gaze upon all mankind and especially upon poor sinners, all enfolded in the Most Compassionate Heart of Jesus. For the sake of His sorrowful Passion, show us Your mercy, that we may praise the omnipotence of Your mercy forever and ever.

In the name of the Father, and of the Son, and of the Holy Spirit. Amen. [21,22]

In 1937, the Divine Mercy image and the Novena grew in popularity as Faustina's health deteriorated and her visions intensified.

Faustina passed away on October 5, 1938 and was laid to rest at the Basilica of Divine Mercy in Krakow, Poland.

Subsequently, in 1965, the Archbishop of Krakow, Karol Wojtyla, who later became Pope John Paul II, submitted documents investigating Faustina's life and virtues to the Vatican, requesting the official beatification process.

This is when the Catholic Church officially declares a deceased person's entrance into Heaven and their ability to intercede on behalf of individuals who pray in their name. It is a step on the path to canonization (sainthood) and entitles the person to the title "Blessed."

She became "Blessed Faustina" on April 18, 1993.

1st Miracle

There were two miracles attributed to Faustina for her sainthood. Maureen Digan of Massachusetts reported a healing in March 1981. She prayed at Faustina's tomb at the Basilica of Divine Mercy in Poland while she suffered from lymphedema, a disease that causes significant swelling and pain from fluid retention. It had plagued her for decades and she had undergone ten operations, including having her leg amputated.

While praying at the tomb, Digas heard a voice saying, "Ask for my help, and I will help you." When she did, her constant pain stopped. Additionally, Digan's said that her foot had been too large for her shoe due to the liquid retention. Two days after the healing, the shoe fit.

When she returned to the United States, five Boston physicians declared her cured. With the testimony of more than 20 additional witnesses, the Vatican declared the case miraculous in 1992.

2nd Miracle

The second miracle was the case of Fr. Pytel. In 1995, Fr. Ron Pytel of Baltimore, Maryland, knew he had bronchitis, he found himself out of breath frequently after climbing a flight of stairs. Upon closer examination, the doctors discovered a massive calcium build-up in his aortic valve. As a result, the left ventricle of his heart had become severely damaged — this is a condition that rarely heals and if it does, it can take several years.

Henceforth, in June of 1995, Fr. Ron had surgery to replace the valve with an artificial one, but the damage to his heart was another problem. When he went for his first regular check-up two months later, the prognosis was not good.

So a world-renowned cardiologist in Baltimore, specified that Fr. Ron's heart would never be normal and that the 48-year-old priest would likely never be able to return to his priestly duties.

However, all of that changed on Oct. 5, 1995 — the Feast Day and 58th anniversary of Saint Faustina's death. After a full day of prayer at his parish, Fr. Ron attended a healing service where he prayed for Saint Faustina's intercession. After venerating her relic, he collapsed on the floor and felt unable to move for about 15 minutes. During his next regular check-up, Fr. Ron's doctor could not explain the condition of the priest's heart — it had returned to normal.

This healing, like all presented to the Catholic Church as "miracles" was thoroughly and exhaustively researched by medical professionals and theologians who deal with the causes for saints.

On Nov. 16, 1999, a panel of doctors declared the healing scientifically unexplainable. The healing was dubbed a miracle by theologians from the Church's Congregation for the Causes of Saints on Dec. 7.

Then, one week later, on Dec. 14, a panel of cardinals and bishops gave their unanimous approval.

Faustina Kowalska became Saint Faustina Kowalska, patron saint of Mercy, on April 30, 2000, under Pope St. John Paul II. Her feast day is celebrated on October 5.

Chapter 17

The Divine Mercy Prayer

He said to them, "When you pray, say: " 'Father, hallowed be your name, your kingdom come. Give us each day our daily bread. Forgive us our sins, for we also forgive everyone who sins against us. And lead us not into temptation. ' " —Luke 11:2 - 4

"I opened my eyes sluggishly, and stared into the sun-filled room as the sunlight splayed across the clean white sheets that covered my bed. I began to absorb my surroundings in the fluorescent rays of the early morning sun. Everything looked unfamiliar, my bedside table littered with stacks of 'Get Well Soon' cards, the threadbare rug scattered with my wearing apparel and an unfamiliar man seated on a wooden armed chair, almost dozing off as he repeated words from the Holy Rosary in desultoriness."

Praying the Rosary

The Divine Mercy Chaplet is to be prayed on the rosary every day at 3 pm, at the hour when Jesus of Nazareth drew his last breath, crying out, "It is finished," as he died on the cross.

It is important that this prayer is not said at 3 am, the Devil's hour, the hour at which Satan mocks Christ. It is the time of Jesus' death flipped to mock Jesus, much like when a cross is turned upside down to symbolize satanism. Remember that the number three is regarded as a holy number within Christianity: the Holy Trinity of the Father, the Son, and the Holy Ghost; Christ's 33 years on earth; the 33 chapters of this book.

The Chaplet of Mercy is recited using an ordinary Rosary with beads of five decades. Before beginning the prayers of the Chaplet, make the sign of the Cross over the cross of the rosary and say, *"In the name of the Father, and of the Son, and of the Holy Spirit. Amen.'*

Before beginning the rosary itself, an optional opening prayer may be said, St. Faustina's Prayer for Sinners, over the first bead of the rosary that is:

Jesus, eternal Truth, our Life. I call upon You and I beg Your mercy for poor Sinners. O sweetest Heart of my Lord, full of pity and unfathomable mercy, I please with You for poor sinners. O Most Sacred Heart, Fount of Mercy from which gush forth rays of inconceivable graces upon the entire human race, I beg of You light for poor sinners.

O Jesus, be mindful of Your own bitter Passion and do not permit the loss of souls redeemed at so dear a price of Your most precious Blood. O Jesus, when I consider the great price of Your Blood, I rejoice at its immensity, for one drop alone would have been enough for the salvation of all sinners.

Although sin is an abyss of wickedness and ingratitude, the price paid for us can never be quelled. Therefore, let every soul trust in the Passion of the Lord, and place its hope in His mercy. God will not deny His mercy to anyone. Heaven and earth may change, but God's mercy will never be exhausted.

Oh, what, immense joy burns in my heart when I contemplate Your incomprehensible goodness. O Jesus! I desire to bring all sinners to Your feet that they may glorify Your mercy through endless ages. (from the Diary of Saint Maria Faustina Kowalska, 72)

You expired, Jesus, but the source of life gushed forth for souls, and the ocean of mercy opened up for the whole world. O Fount of Life, unfathomable Divine Mercy, envelop the whole world and empty Yourself out upon us.

O Blood and Water, which gushed forth from the Heart of Jesus as a fount of mercy for us, I trust in You! (Repeat three times) (Say your intentions)

Then the Our Father is prayed over the next bead, the beginning of a set of three beads:

Our Father, Who art in heaven, hallowed be Thy name; Thy kingdom come; Thy will be done as earth as it is in heaven. Give us this day our daily bread; and forgive us our trespasses as we forgive those who trespass against us; and lead us not into temptation, but deliver us from evil. Amen.

Now pray the Hail Mary over the third bead above the cross:

Hail Mary, full of grace. The Lord is with thee. Blessed art thou amongst women and blessed is the fruit of thy womb, Jesus. Holy Mary, Mother of God, pray for us sinners, now and at the hour of our death. Amen.

On the final bead of the set of three, pray the Apostles' Creed:

I believe in God, the Father almighty, Creator of heaven and earth, and in Jesus Christ, His only Son, our Lord, who has conceived by the Holy Spirit, born of the Virgin Mary, suffered under Pontius Pilate, was crucified, died and was buried; He descended into hell; on the third day He rose again from the dead; he ascended into heaven, and is seated at the right hand of God the Father almighty; from there He will come to judge the living and the dead. I believe in the Holy Spirit, the holy catholic Church, the communion of saints, the forgiveness of sins, the resurrection of the body, and life everlasting. Amen.

Prayed on large bead prior to the juncture and the beginning of the decade beads (sets of ten)

Eternal Father, I offer you the Body and Blood, Soul and Divinity of Your Dearly Beloved Son, Our Lord, Jesus Christ, in atonement for our sins and those of the whole world.[10]

Prayed on 10 small beads of each decade

For the sake of His sorrowful Passion, have mercy on us and on the whole world.

Prayed after all 5 decades of Chaplet are complete

Holy God, Holy Mighty One, Holy Immortal One, have mercy on us and on the whole world. (Repeat three times.)

There is then an optional closing prayer:

Eternal God, in whom mercy is endless and the treasury of compassion – inexhaustible, look kindly upon us and increase Your mercy in us, that in difficult moments we might not despair nor become despondent, but with great confidence submit ourselves to Your holy will, which is Love and Mercy itself.

O Greatly Merciful God, Infinite Goodness, today all mankind calls out from the abyss of its misery to Your mercy – to Your compassion, O God; and it is with its mighty voice of misery that it cries out. Gracious God, do not reject the prayer of this earth's exiles! O Lord, Goodness beyond our understanding, Who is acquainted with our misery through and through, and know that by our own power we cannot ascend to You, we implore You:

anticipate us with Your grace and keep on increasing Your mercy in us, that we may faithfully do Your holy will all through our life and at death's hour. Let the omnipotence of Your mercy shield us from the darts of our salvation's enemies, that we may with confidence, as Your children, await Your Son's final coming – that day known to You alone. And we expect to obtain everything promised us by Jesus in spite of all our wretchedness. For Jesus is our Hope: through His merciful Heart, as through an open gate, we pass through to heaven. (from the Diary of Saint Maria Faustina Kowalska, 1570)

Chapter 18

Dad Arrives

He implored Him earnestly, saying, "My little daughter is at the point of death; please come and lay Your hands on her, so that she will get well and live." —Mark 5:23

"I needed fresh air; I needed to get rid of the insane delusion that something terrible had happened! And I was actually on earth, though my encounter with the Lord was thus enthralling.

I languidly dragged myself out of my warm bed, slipped my feet into my shoes, walked on the pile of clothes that lay scattered on the floor and felt the need to slide through the enormous gray door. I slinked out of the door and walked on my tiptoes on the soft pads of my shoe soles onto a meddlesome, assiduous area that looked like systematic living quarters".

Must I say Goodbye?

While my father waited for his visa so he could fly to be with me in Australia, he and my mum were frequently and frantically calling either the hospital or my host family for any updates. Naturally, it was their nightmare to have their oldest child, who had traveled to the other side of the world to begin her future, meet a tragic accident – hit by a car driven by an inattentive student behind the wheel.

The host family visited me in the hospital, where I was surrounded by a team of medical professionals. "She doesn't have long to live. Get her family here ASAP," they kept telling the couple.

X-Rays and other tests were conducted on my internal organs and the doctors and nurses were sure they knew my fate – no chance of survival.

Repeatedly, my father would ask people who were near me, "Is there a white chair next to her hospital bed? I keep seeing one there."

No one really understood his illusions and ignored the question, choosing instead to focus on any updates they knew about, though they were generally the same –hopeless, 'I would not recover.'

At last, the visa came through and my father arrived in Melbourne after a long flight. He was HERE; on Saturday, the 17th of February, he was with his nearly dying daughter.

The host family met him at the airport. They immediately drove to the hospital, where he spotted the white chair next to my hospital bed. It confirmed in his heart that the Lord had never left my side and had conveyed His careful watch over me all those many miles to my father.

The doctors told him that I had experienced a traumatic brain injury – a TBI. The injuries I had sustained included a broken right hip and a punctured lung and I was currently brain dead. In the three days I had been in the hospital, there had been no improvement.

My father stood at my side, looking down at his oldest child lying lifeless on a cold hospital bed. Tubes ran through parts of my body, starting at my head. They ran down my side, in both my hands, into my nose and my mouth. I was covered in bruises and lacerations and there were cuts over most of my face.

"Most patients in this state, a level three of neurological damage, remain in a vegetative state if they survive at all. We strongly advise you to prepare a eulogy," the doctors told my father. "Get the rest of the family here to say their goodbyes, if you possibly can. If you're a religious family, now is the time to bring a priest to perform the last rites.

…Before it's too late," the doctor said.

The medical team told my father that I might never wake up from the coma that left me lying pale on the white sheets. If I did awaken, it could be six to eight months before my brain came to anything resembling normal. I would probably never recover all of my memories. Or recognize familiar faces. All due to the horrific impact on that fateful day as I walked out of a milk bar.

As my father collapsed under the weight of the information, he felt as though he would suffocate from the idea that he might lose me. Crying uncontrollably, he prayed over my lifeless body, pouring his heart to God. Even as questions raced through his head, his faith kept him going. Each time his resolve weakened, he turned his mind to the Lord and prayed for strength. He took my hand in his as he sat in the white chair next to my bed and prayed out loud over me, "Oh Lord, hear my prayer, as you raised Lazarus from the dead in four days, you will raise my daughter too from this mere mortal accident."

JOHN 11, 1-24

A man named Lazarus was sick. He lived in Bethany with his sisters, Mary and Martha. This is the Mary who later poured the expensive perfume on the Lord's feet and wiped them with her hair. Her brother, Lazarus, was sick. So the two sisters sent a message to Jesus telling him, "Lord, your dear friend is very sick."

But when Jesus heard about it, he said, "Lazarus's sickness will not end in death. No, it happened for the glory of God so that the Son of God will receive glory from this." So although Jesus loved Martha, Mary, and Lazarus, he stayed where he was for the next two days. Finally, he said to his disciples, "Let's go back to Judea."

But his disciples objected. "Rabbi," they said, "only a few days ago, the people in Judea were trying to stone you. Are you going there again?"

Jesus replied, "There are twelve hours of daylight every day. During the day, people can walk safely. They can see because they have the light of this world. But at night, there is a danger of stumbling because they have no light." Then he said, "Our friend Lazarus has fallen asleep, but now I will go and wake him up."

The disciples said, "Lord, if he is sleeping, he will soon get better!" They thought Jesus meant Lazarus was simply sleeping, but Jesus meant Lazarus had died.

So he told them plainly, "Lazarus is dead. And for your sake, I'm glad I wasn't there, for now, you will really believe. Come, let's go see him."

Thomas, nicknamed the Twin and said to his fellow disciples, "Let's go, too—and die with Jesus."

When Jesus arrived at Bethany, he was told that Lazarus had already been in his grave for four days. Bethany was only a few miles down the road from Jerusalem, and many of the people had come to console Martha and Mary in their loss. When Martha got word that Jesus was coming, she went to meet him. But Mary stayed in the house. Martha said to Jesus, "Lord, if only you had been here, my brother would not have died.

But even now, I know that God will give you whatever you ask."

Jesus told her, "I am the resurrection and the life. Anyone who believes in me will live, even after dying. Everyone who lives in me and believes in me will never ever die. Do you believe this, Martha?"

Yes, Lord," she told him. "I have always believed you are the Messiah, the Son of God, the one who has come into the world from God.

When Jesus saw her weeping and saw the other people wailing with her, a deep anger welled up within him and he was deeply troubled. "Where have you put him?" he asked them.

They told him, "Lord, come and see." Then Jesus wept. The people who were standing nearby said, "See how much he loved him!" But some said, "This man healed a blind man. Couldn't he have kept Lazarus from dying?"

Jesus was still angry as he arrived at the tomb, a cave with a stone rolled across its entrance. "Roll the stone aside," Jesus told them.

But Martha, the dead man's sister, protested, "Lord, he has been dead for four days. The smell will be terrible."

Jesus responded, "Didn't I tell you that you would see God's glory if you believe?" So they rolled the stone aside. Then Jesus looked up to heaven and said, "Father, thank you for hearing me. You always hear me, but I said it out loud for the sake of all these people standing here so that they will believe you sent me." Then Jesus shouted, "Lazarus, come out!" And the dead man came out, his hands and feet bound in grave clothes, his face wrapped in a head cloth. Jesus told them, "Unwrap him and let him go!"

Chapter 19

Alfred Hospital and Monash University

Now Isaiah had said, "Let them take a cake of figs and apply it to the boil, that he may recover." —Isaiah 38:21

"There were ecstatic cheers from a seventy-two-year-old across my room, as people clapped around him and nurses nodded and there I stood with a faraway look, having no clue to what was happening or why I was here."

So I whizzed around the corner; I noticed people with broken arms and legs and thankfully, I thought nothing had happened to me.

Among the cheers, shouts and misery, I returned to my island of solitude on earth!

The Teaching Hospital

Alfred Hospital, also known as "The Alfred," is a leading tertiary teaching hospital in connection with Monash University. While it is the oldest Melbourne hospital that still operates on its original site, it is the second oldest hospital in Victoria. Being one of two major adult trauma centers in Victoria with the largest intensive care unit in Australia, it was the only choice for me to be airlifted to.

Plans were already being made to establish a second hospital in Victoria when Prince Alfred, Duke of Edinburgh, was in the area on a royal visit. An assassination attempt was made on his life when he was shot. Thus, the "hospital by the Yarra" was named after him when it was founded in 1871.

The Alfred Hospital offers numerous specialty services, including treatment for cancer, asthma, psychiatry, allergies, cardiology, and neurosurgery. It has the largest intensive care unit in Australia as well as the only adult burn center in Victoria and Tasmania, and the only Adult Heart and Lung transplant service in Victoria (which is the second largest in the world), and the only Pediatric Lung transplant service in all of Australia. Clearly, it is a hospital at the forefront of medical treatment.

Shortly before this book was written, in 2021, The Alfred Hospital was ranked as one of the world's best hospitals.

Chapter 20

Mass is the Central Act of the Catholic Faith

Therefore I say unto you, What things soever ye desire, when ye pray, believe that ye receive them, and ye shall have them. **—Mark 11:24**

"On the 14th day after my accident, my father noticed I was not aware of what had happened as he watched me flip through each card, ascertained, he did not interrupt. In my oppressive gloom, I snatched a glimpse of him and tried to detect his facial expressions.

Reading through my pain, his thoughts began to surface; he hesitated for a brief moment and then asked me. "Do you feel any pain" "No, I don't, I feel perfectly normal" I said. A sob of relief led my father to dial a few buttons on his mobile phone as he grabbed it from the edge where the Holy Bible lay".

The Holy Mass

It was the next day; my father spent an afternoon reminiscing through the chapters of the Holy Bible before making his way to church. He seemed calmer when he arrived at the church and before he took his seat, he prayed with sincerity at a Mother Mary statue before he sat down.

It was a Sunday, and my father dutifully attended mass.

Around the world, Mass has been celebrated pretty much the same for over 2000 years. In most catholic churches, a parishioner dips their right hand into a bowl of holy water at the entrance and makes the sign of the cross on their forehead. This ritual is a reminder of Baptism when they were baptized with water. To honor the altar and the presence of Christ in the tabernacle, they sign with the cross before entering the pew.

The congregation stands while waiting for the priest to walk in and the mass to begin. They sing the entrance hymn while he gets ready to start the mass. The priest turns to the congregation and leads them in signing the cross, reminding them again of their Baptism in their faith.

"The Lord be with you," he says. And they reply, "And also with you."

Mass is the central act of Catholic life. It is the holiest act we have here on earth because it is the action of Christ. It is not primarily about what is read from the Holy Scriptures, even though that is the word of God and should be listened to and learned from as such. It is not either primarily what the priest preaches in his sermon or about what the people do or sing. It is about what Christ does.

The act of Christ offering himself to us, as he offered Himself on the Cross, as he Sacrificed Himself for us. In this case, He offers himself on the altar, His body and blood, as he did on the Cross, in an unbloodied manner. Where they were visible on the Cross for those present to see, in the Mass, they are hidden in the bread and the wine, though our faith tells us they are truly present.

The Holy Eucharist is the 'mystery of faith." It is faith that accepts that when the priest says, "This is my body" and "This is the cup of my blood," the bread and the wine become the true embodiment of Christ's body and blood. Without faith, they are simply a gesture, a symbol, and nothing more.

While praying, a Catholic should have 'the same mind' as Christ had on the cross (*Let this mind be in you which was also in Christ Jesus* — Philippians 2:5).

That begins the adoration of God, that He is infinite, eternal, all-powerful. If God Almighty is all-powerful, there is nothing He cannot do, no one He cannot heal.

Thoughts similar to these ran through my father's head as he prayed with all his mind and soul that day in a church at Springvale.

In keeping with Christ's thoughts on the Cross, a Catholic should give thanks. God is infinitely good and all the good things we have come from Him. I still had my life.

However fragile it was, my father was going to witness the biggest miracle right in front of him on the day.

So as worship continued……

A part of the Holy Mass is the penitential act, the "I confess" that is said together at the start of the Mass. It does not pardon mortal sin – that forgiveness must be obtained in the sacrament of penance, and a person who has committed one cannot go to communion unless he has gone to confession beforehand. But the penitential act, said with conviction, helps obtain pardon for present venial sins and helps purify us to take part in the Holy Mass.

And finally, the parishioner asks the Lord to grant his prayer. "*Ask and ye shall receive.*" **John 16:24**. This is most effective when we can back up our petition with a belief in our special merit, but often we feel we are so full of defects that we see no reason why

God should fulfill our petition. That is why we unite our prayer with that of Jesus.

God the Father will always hear the prayer of his beloved Son, who prayed for us on the cross and continues to pray for us on the altar.

In this way, my father prayed for me.

While he prayed, my father heard a voice speaking to him. He distinctly heard the voice say, "She will talk to you." Being a man of strong faith, he accepted and embraced it! He strongly believed it would happen.

When the mass had concluded, he simply knelt in front of the Eucharist, tears rolling down his cheeks as he continued to pray. "Lord," he prayed. "You are Miraculous, You are merciful; I will never stop believing."

The host family who had accompanied him to mass sat beside him all that while and listened to some of the words uttered out loud. They obviously did believe my father was experiencing a delusional disorder and could have misinterpreted his perception after being told he was spoken to by a voice, most likely Mother Mary's voice.

"A voice spoke to me today and told me, 'Your daughter will talk to you.' I know it was our dearest Mother Mary," my father said to him.

The host husband, an atheist, a faithless man, turned to my father and said, "I don't mean to be rude," …a statement which generally proceeds a statement the speaker clearly knows will, in fact, be quite rude… "but you heard what the doctor told you just yesterday that if Colette ever comes around, perhaps in a few months, since she is currently very much in a coma, she won't recognize you or anyone. So you have experienced hallucinations, which is completely understandable for someone whose daughter has been given a short time to live. ”

"I know what the doctor said," my father calmly replied, "But I also know my Lord turns the impossible situation into the possible situation.

"Faith is, after all, the 'substance of things hoped for, the evidence of things not seen.' Hebrews 11:1."

Arguments passed back and forth between the believer and the non-believer on the drive to the hospital.

And walking into the emergency room, my father noticed the shunts on my head had been removed.

Chapter 21

Lord, Hear My Prayer

This day I call the heavens and the earth as witnesses against you that I have set before you life and death, blessings and curses. Now choose life, so that you and your children may live. —Deuteronomy 30:19

"I did have a short encounter with our Lord. I did see him!

A thud, flapping sound and vibrations came down from above and I wondered if the shimmering beings I saw earlier at a distance were the ones producing it.

Then I heard a gentle whisper in my ear: "Come, with me," the voice said. So I opened my eyes, but there was no one in that hospital room. But I knew what I heard was real. I looked around again to see if I missed anything and there stood a purely white figure with an enormous smile with open arms towards me."

Signs of Improvement

On the 7th day at the hospital, my respirator had been turned off and the breathing tube extracted. The incision on my sides did not look as swollen as the previous day. My father was yet to be informed that my brain swelling was in control and the tube had been removed from my head too.

"What's going on?" My father asked one of the nurses scurrying about the hospital. "My daughter's shunt has been removed. Does that mean she's improving?"

"Give me a moment. I'll have to check her chart," the nurse replied, carefully not giving hope where none was justified.

To my father, the time she took to peruse my file seemed eternal, though he knew it was only moments. He had to force himself to remain calm, not to lean his head over her shoulder to read the words for himself.

Finally, she turned to him. "It seems Colette's brain has normalized in the past 24 hours. The shunt will no longer be required." She gave my father a brief, reassuring smile.

"Oh my Lord, that is absolutely incredible to hear", my father replied, contently smiling through it all. There was more than a sigh of relief, his shoulders dropped and for the first time in 7 days, the weight lifted off them.

The heavens had heard his prayers and had begun to answer them.

He slipped into the white chair next to my bed that he had seen in his dreams. Holding up my hand as gently as possible, he just sat there for a few minutes, content in this small victory.

Then a doctor came into the room to check on my status. They conversed a bit and the doctor noted my improvement.

When the doctor left the room, my father picked up his rosary and began to pray.

It felt like the beginning of the end. He sat there reciting one rosary after the next and gently laid his hands on my head. He then put an ointment on my lips to reduce the swelling and the cracking as they were bleeding. He cried while he prayed.

On each bead, he said, "Hail Mary, full of grace, the Lord is with you. Bless are you among women and blessed is the fruit of thy womb, Jesus. Holy Mary, Mother of God, pray for the outpouring of the Holy Spirit on Colette." He moved to the next bead and repeated the prayer. Then he did it again. My father spent the entire day praying over me, watching me twitch as he prayed, believing in a miracle.

"If I were you, I would appeal to God; I would lay my cause before him. He performs wonders that cannot be fathomed, miracles that cannot be counted." Job 5:8-9

Chapter 22

The Ninth Day
After the Accident

Heal me, LORD, and I will be healed; save me and I will be saved, for you are the one I praise. —Jeremiah 17:14

"Does heaven exist? Yes, it does, only because I envisioned it. I knew it simply was not just a dream. I was taken to a heavenly dimension where I saw people standing with their hands uplifted in praise and glorifying God. When I looked to my right, I saw a gold throne, but it was empty....

I looked to my left; I saw many angelic apparitions, some with their wings open and some that knelt down. There were also quite a few water fountains all around that had crystal clear water and did not have an end to their stream. There were bright green fluorescent trees with colourful flowers that sat on a white cloud in the distance.`

Joyful, Joyful, and Amen

By Wednesday, a week and one day after my accident, to the doctor's surprise, my brain had normalized even more. "We can see additional improvement," they explained to my father after yet more testing. Every day there were tests. My father clapped his hands together in joy.

Thursday, nine days after the accident, the nurses removed the tube from my lungs on the doctor's orders. "This is not the usual progress," one of them told my father. "It must be your prayers," she said with her lilting Australian accent.

"Hallelujah," my father replied, his hands together in supplication. To the nurse, he was the one with an accent.

Was this the day my father's prayers were answered?

What seemed medically impossible seemed possible with God!

So as the day progressed, I became more stable and more comfortable with the respirator out and breathing well on my own. The swelling had largely subsided.

There had been significant improvement overnight. My punctured lung and damaged liver had normalized in a matter of a few days! My right hip had fixed itself and though the tubes that fed my digestive system were not removed yet, there had been a miraculous recovery.

Then he buried his head in his hands, his heart filled with hope and longing in his prayer.

And he remembered the words Mary had spoken to him, "SHE WILL TALK TO YOU"!

As he touched my forehead, making the sign of the cross.....

In less than 30 seconds, I was wide awake and sat upright on the bed and summoned my father saying, "Daddy, you've come. Take me home!".

All of a sudden, all around, there was a blur of grinning, lurching faces, my voice like a second pulse, the exclamation remarks of the nurses, the doctors stunned and everything coming to a pause, like they had witnessed something extraordinary.

"She's awake!" There were whispers in the hallway. Nurses came running to peek over each other's shoulders from the hallway. "It's a miracle." "He's been praying for days." Some mumbled prayers of their own. Others crossed themselves.

My doctor pushed his way through the crowd so that he could examine me. He put his stethoscope to my heart. He examined where the shunt had been in my head. He took my pulse, examined my wounds, gazed into my eyes, poked and prodded. Then he stood back and simply stared.

"It's MIRACULOUS," he finally pronounced in a whisper. He cleared his throat. "I don't know how else to explain it. "Nine days ago, she was brain dead. Now, she is awake. And *speaking*." He turned to my father. "It's truly miraculous."

The other doctors and the nurses gathered in the hallway began to applaud. "The miracle man," they called my father.

The next day, Friday a few of the scabs on my face gently fell away on their own. My father wondered if his once beautiful daughter would be scarred for life, but luckily it was all nearly off.

It is difficult for me to call myself beautiful, coming from a country where women are raised to be modest. But when I look back at the photographs of my 19-year-old self, I see a girl with perfect, youthful skin; her black hair flowing down her back; her eyes are bright and shining with the new world of promise opening before her was now all coming back to her, coming back to me!

Every day I made slow progress. Initially, I was in a confusional state and barely remembered my family members. There were days I had difficulty paying attention and recalling names, other days, I felt agitated, nervous and restless. From a ward in the ICU, I was transferred to a normal ward at the hospital.

Comprehending the Specifics of TBI (Traumatic Brain Injury)

Often, the fastest improvement happens in the first six months after injury.

During this time, I can either move and think better or my speed of improvement can slow down, but this varies from person to person and it is also possible that I can gain more function years after the injury.

There are possible effects of Traumatic Brain Injury even after many years and scans conducted do not always show the full extent of the brain injury.

My injury was severe and the medical experts were unsure of my recovery or long-term existence.

Research from the TBI Model System program, at 2 years after injury, say: from severe to moderate TBI:

1. *About 30% of people need some amount of assistance from another person. This may be during the day, at night, or both. Over time, most people can move around again without help. They can also take care of themselves. This includes bathing and dressing.*

2. *Trouble with thinking is common. This includes how fast a person can think. It also includes forming new memories. The severity of these problems varies.*

3. *About 25% of people have major depression. In some cases, it's caused directly by brain injury. In addition, people with*

TBI are also dealing with major changes in their lives caused by the trauma, including changes in employment, driving, and living circumstances.

4. *Just over 90% of people live in a private home. Of those who were living alone when they were injured, almost half go back to living alone.*

5. *About 50% of people can drive again, but there may be changes in how often they drive or when.*

6. *About 30% of people have a job, but it may not be the same job they had before the injury. Many people get help from vocational rehabilitation counselors who help people with TBI and other disabilities to go back to work.[5]*

Chapter 23

Miracle Man

By faith in the name of Jesus, this man whom you see and know was made strong. It is Jesus' name and the faith that comes through him that has completely healed him, as you can all see. —Acts 3:16

"The light was so bright, it hurt my eyes, so I put my hand over them to cover it, but it got brighter....I felt a cold rush down my spine and that is when I cleared my throat and asked, "Who are you?" in childlike awe and wonder.

Without using any words, he spoke to me. The message read "You have nothing to fear".

"You are beyond loved and cherished. "Follow me whenever I call you".

Miraculous

No one could believe what had just happened. Everyone was shocked and amazed. It had only been nine days when they had expected my recovery to take six months just for me to come out of my coma.

"Will you pray over me?" A nurse asked my father. At first, he was shocked. Then, he took out his rosary and calmly said a prayer with her. Later, another nurse snuck in between patients. "Pray for me," she begged.

The doctor returned, hauling another doctor with him. "You just won't believe it," he whispered. "I am myself in awe of her incredible recovery. It can only be through the grace of God. I have never seen medicine perform such a miracle. And the man has been here praying for nine days. What do you think?

The other doctor simply nodded his head. What else could he do?

And my father prayed on and glorified the Lord.

* * *

The host family that I had lived with before my accident, the husband, known as the atheist.

Who also argued religion with my father initially, witnessed my miracle at the hospital, and couldn't believe what he had just observed.

He promised to visit the Divine Retreat Center. True to his word, a year later, he did.

I spoke more. The tubes feeding into my stomach were removed so I could begin to slowly eat and drink physically. Soft foods only at first. I quickly showed significant improvement. But my long-term memory did not improve, to begin with.

Still, my father was not discouraged. He spoke about my mother, my siblings, Calvin and Charisma, and other things that would remind me of my home in Calcutta.

He arranged for me to have conversations with my family via speakerphone almost every day.

111

They had to be brief because I would get tired so easily. But my mother was thrilled to hear my voice, even for those few brief moments.

My progress was so rapid that I only needed to spend a few days in the emergency ward, where I awoke from my induced coma before being transferred into the main ward. And only three more days in the hospital before I was transferred to a rehabilitation center where I spent the bulk of my recovery.

This stage of recovery may last days or even weeks for some people. In this stage of recovery, ups and downs are normal and are not cause for concern.

My behavior was Inconsistent, which was apparently common for someone who had experienced a traumatic head injury. Some days are better than others.

To this day, I have no recollection of my days in the hospital. The reason being that the type of brain injury I had suffered caused a type of cognitive symptom and an impairment that left out most of the incident. This also happens because the swelling from the trauma puts pressure on the brain, restricting the flow of information. Only when there is a decrease in swelling may this result in the return of memories. Or even sometimes, individual experiences can cause torn fibers in the brain that are no longer able to make appropriate connections and memories, which is a complete loss of memory.

Individuals commonly experience forgetfulness after a car accident as a symptom of a serious head injury. Forgetfulness could be the direct result of a car accident, especially accidents where an individual strikes their head on the windshield, steering wheel or other parts of the car. Individuals suffering from these types of injuries can experience forgetfulness at any stage of the injury and even during the healing process.

Injuries ranging from a mild concussion to a serious brain injury can result in an individual experiencing a myriad of forgetfulness and other memory loss issues.

When an individual is in a car accident, swelling from the trauma can put pressure on the brain, restricting the flow of information. While often a decrease in swelling will result in the return of memories, for some individuals, memories may never resurface. When an individual experiences torn fibers in the brain that can no longer make the appropriate connections to access memories, a complete loss of memory may ensue.

Many individuals who suffer from forgetfulness after a car accident experience what is known as post-traumatic amnesia (PTA). PTA is a state of confusion or loss of memory immediately after a traumatic event like a car accident. This generally occurs when an individual is involved in a car accident that results in a traumatic brain injury from a blow to the head. **Anterograde amnesia** *is the most common type of memory loss that is reported after an accident. Anterograde amnesia happens when an individual is unable to remember the events that occur following a car accident. As a result of an incorrect encoding in the brain, memories that are lost due to anterograde amnesia are never regained.*

Another type of amnesia commonly suffered by car accident victims is **retrograde amnesia.** *An individual suffering from retrograde amnesia experiences the loss of memories that are formed before a traumatic head injury.*[16]

Chapter 24

Sixteen Days

Wherefore he saith, Awake thou that sleepest, and arise from the dead, and Christ shall give thee light.
—Ephesians 5:14

"Was It Jesus??!!

This message flooded me and mesmerized me! It was so distinctive and just when a warm wind blew through, a divine breeze!

It was an exhilarating sense of excitement and compulsion that transformed in me, sending shivers through my spine. I couldn't believe it!"

Take Me Home

I set off on a slow-paced walk around the obstructed space and wondered how I came in here in the first place.

I looked around. *Where am I?* I wondered. Everything looked unfamiliar and I remembered…nothing. Nothing at all. My feet ached. As I became aware of the pain, I realized my knees hurt, too. My consciousness worked its way up my body. Oh, the ache included my torso – part of my face, my chin, and my arms!

Where am I? How did I get here? What happened? Why do I hurt?!? I had so many questions, but no words came out of my mouth. They didn't even reach my mouth.

I scanned the room to see if I could tell where I was. My mind was beginning to function past the pain in my body. It was sparse, that room. Sterile.

There was a big man who seemed to be sleeping in an armchair next to my bed. He was middle-aged, clutching a rosary in his hands. *Should I ask him who I am? Why am I here? Why does it hurt!*

Something terrible has happened, I thought to myself. *Why else would there be so much pain?* I moaned as I tried to stretch out my arms and legs. They felt as though I hadn't used them in years. I had no idea it had only been nine days. I also didn't know I had been hit by a 700 kg (around 1540 lbs) car. My body ached as I hadn't moved it in a while. My head throbbed. But worst of all, I couldn't remember anything.

On the table beside me, I also spotted a glass of water, so with a painful stretch, I reached for it. As I grabbed it, the strange man in the chair beside me awoke. When he opened his eyes, I recognized his face. *How could I not have known him before? It was my father.*

Why was he here? Why was I here?

I walked around for less than 5 minutes and then turned around and asked my father the big question.

"How did I get here?" my raspy voice squeaked out.

Reading through my worrisome look, his thoughts began to surface; he hesitated for a brief moment and then asked me. "Can you remember anything?" No, maybe, I don't know, I replied flustered.

He then asked me to sit comfortably and began his narration.

Chapter 25

The Victorian Rehabilitation Center

Every good and perfect gift is from above, coming down from the Father of the heavenly lights, who does not change like shifting shadows. —James 1:17

"When the immaculate figure looked at me with absolutely no expression on his face. He then pointed to the vital signs monitor above my head and smiled. I looked at it confused and looked back at him.

Before I knew it, the infographic monitor beeps several times."

Memories Are Elusive

I was moved to The Victorian Rehabilitation Center in Glen Waverley, Victoria, Australia. It is a dedicated private rehabilitation provider in Melbourne's southeast. It was here that I one day woke up and asked my father what had happened to me. Taking his time, he told me everything he knew about the accident, how I had been hit by a car, that I had been outside the milk bar on my way back to the host family's house from the

University. He told me that emergency measures had been taken on me to save my life before I had been airlifted away from the scene to Alfred Hospital, where I was pronounced brain dead. He also told me that he had been told that I wouldn't survive, that the family needed to say their goodbyes.

I couldn't believe what I was hearing. It all seemed so unreal. I had no memory of being hit by a car. How could that happen and I couldn't remember any of it? At all.

I struggled to remember something and as my thoughts triggered back to the accident.

I slowly…	Remembered stepping out of the university campus, sniffing the deep cool, clean air as the evening rays had set in and the sky to the west still offered defiant rays to the late sun.
When…she asked…..	"Do you want a ride home Colette?". "No, thank you, I should be alright", I replied.

Elaina could see it in tumult, in the creases of my frown and pursed lips.

It was the train station across the street that appeared to be the source of my distress.

AND then. There were three blocks left until I reached the end of my predetermined journey.

Two blocks, and I felt ravenous as I could hear my hunger pangs rumble within. One block had I completed when… there was an occurrence of a head-on

COLLUSION!!!....................

BANG!!!! The car slammed round the bend, the two front parts of its progression, of rubber, screeched into the lamp post...............................

From then on, I tried, but there just wasn't anything else I could recall.

Not until I woke up in the rehabilitation center with my father at my side.

My father then went on to tell me about the religious side of things and how he had prayed. And prayed. And prayed. It was miraculous.

I had recovered so soon, and I knew full well how extraordinary and unbelievable this experience was. Not even doctors could fathom my recovery. They were all certain my father was under some sort of delusion. But my miraculous recovery was far from delusional.

* * *

Though I had no memory of my days in the hospital, my long life memory before the accident slowly started to return. I couldn't remember things from the present.

Loss of short-term memory, that is, a memory of fewer than 30 minutes, seems to be a rather common side effect of Traumatic Brain Injury, although many people have other memory loss, including amnesia from TBI as well. I was fortunate to begin recalling memories from a decade earlier.

My two friends from my first day – my only day – at the university came to visit me: Eliana and Devi. I was not too thrilled about their visit because I wasn't in my best attire and I didn't recognize them. It wasn't until about two months later that my memory of how I met them began to slowly come back, and I started to remember bits and pieces of university and Eliana and Devi and everyone else I met on the day of my orientation.

Initially, my father had to remind me of who they were. I'm sure it was as embarrassing for them as it was for me.

Rehabilitation

My days at the rehabilitation center became a routine. I had well-being therapy sessions. These are mental health sessions designed to encourage positive thinking through cognitive restructuring. When I identified episodes of well-being, I wrote them in a diary so that I could recall them later if I caught myself thinking in negative ways that discouraged healing or caused distress. This therapy also included activities that elicited well-being and positive, purposeful, and meaningful growth. Under the trying circumstances of the physical and emotional recovery from such a traumatic event, a person is vulnerable to depression and anxiety. For me, turning to prayer with my father's encouragement helped bring a positive and healthy spirituality to enlighten my mentality.

I also underwent physiotherapy, moving my limbs and my body to help restore my body's movements to their pre-accident condition and to strengthen my muscles. It also improved my coordination. I also conversed with a speech therapist.

After a brain injury, speech patterns can often change. Even the quality of breathiness can be changed. Often TBI patients have slurred speech or develop a stutter. Speech therapy helps prevent or correct such difficulties.

And, of course, I met with the psychiatrist at least once a week, who encouraged me to talk about my feelings as well as to write them down. She told me to keep up a positive attitude, which could be quite challenging.

We also discussed books I had read, which were mostly Sydney Sheldon, as he was my favorite author back then. Now I read anything from fiction to nonfiction and everything or whatever tickles my fancy. So one of the books I read at rehab was Sydney Sheldon's "If Tomorrow Comes." It's a crime fiction novel portraying an affluent woman, pregnant and in love, framed by the Mafia. She is sent to prison for a crime she didn't commit. When she is released, she seeks vengeance against those who put her there and caused her mother's suicide. The quest leads her across the globe.

The psychiatrist asked probing questions about the plot to assess whether or not I had comprehended what I read. How was my brain working? If I could go back to starting University? At that stage, I was still a high school graduate. Was I still thinking, processing like one? Or had my brain's logic centers been affected by the impact of the accident? My understanding of Sheldon's novel gave the psychiatrist an indication of just how well my brain had fared. It seemed prayers had been answered well and thoroughly.

Dad Must Depart

Some days, it was difficult waiting for my father to arrive at the rehabilitation center since he could only be with me during visiting hours, 8 am to 8 pm. Often, I would pass the time reading books from its library. I really valued the time we spent together.

Unfortunately, my father finally had to return home. He stayed with me until the 5th of March because his well-established restaurant business, Sher-E-Punjab, demanded his attention and he had to go back to attend to it. When he left, I became homesick and desperately wanted to return home where I would have my loving family to support me before I went back to my studies. Anticipating returning to University gave me a reason to keep going. Being alone, so lonely, made me depressed. I constantly fought depression after my father left.

But they would not let me leave the rehabilitation center until they saw significant improvement. Their reasons for keeping me there were valid, but even with the regular phone conversations with my family back home, I felt such emptiness. I was alone in a far-away country with no one I knew or loved near me. I had started out just two months earlier on an exciting journey that had been predicted as a life-changing miracle for me. I had seen that in such a positive light. "God is going to work through you," the priest had said in distinctive words. He had assured me that the only right decision was to go to Melbourne for my studies. I had done that. And look at where it had gotten me – bloodied and broken and alone in a strange land with no one I loved to take care of me. I had to blink back the tears and pick up my journal of well-being.

Chapter 26

Nicholas

Commit to the Lord whatever you do, and He will establish your plans — Proverbs 16:3

"I trust in You Lord, " I repeated these words as I closed my eyes, again. Before I knew it, the screen glowed brighter and the info on the monitor made a sound warning. There was this loud beeping noise and a flashing colour; the oxygen in my blood lowered!

Nurses and doctors rushed in."

Nicholas – People of Victory

It was lonely and depressing in the hospital. For all the patients. Even if you are a local because friends and family could only visit during visiting hours. Nick had no family. And only a few friends.

Nick and I were drawn to each other, in part, because we are close in age. He was just 9 months my senior. Nick was born in February, and I in December of the same year.

Since my father left, I formed my own little anxious bubble, and during this time, I developed a friendship with Nick, who made me forget my anxiousness and dwell in positivity.

Nick's accident happened a few weeks before mine, on January 27, 2007.

Partially intoxicated, he was walking home from a friend's party a little after midnight. Crossing the road in a random place rather than at the appropriate pedestrian crossing, he was hit by a car traveling at 70 km per hour. A woman was behind the wheel. That's all he knows about the car.

He was unconscious at the scene and sustained a head injury just like myself. He was in a coma for a few weeks before he came around. He also broke both ankles. Both had to have metal plates put into them. Till today he still has pain in them from time to time, especially after standing for long periods.

He wasn't so lucky after his accident. He ended up in a wheelchair for a time because he had to have metal plates in both ankles for support which prevented him from walking for a few months until they set and healed. After some time, he was able to walk on crutches. Then eventually, without them.

We gelled; Nick quickly became my only friend at rehab, even though he was the opposite of spiritual, and everyone seemed to be warning us away from each other. One of the psychologists who talked individually with each of the patients once or twice a week didn't seem to be much of a Nick fan. She warned me to stay away from him, to not even talk to him as a friend but to keep to myself.

Her words, "He might influence you to make wrong decisions," the psychiatrist said.

Often psychiatrists in wards warn patients to keep to themselves so that their mental states are not influenced by anyone but the staff. Other patients may become depressed by their current predicament – pain, frustration with their slow recovery, or even fail to remember (due to head trauma which both me and Nick were experiencing) what they had said or done the day before –

and act out or negatively influence another patient they have the opportunity to intimately converse with.

The psychiatrist knew, from meeting my father, that I came from an elite family and that I was a university student with hopes and dreams and unseen potential ahead of me.

She had spoken with my father and knew that he owned his own business and had a bright future planned for me.

The psychiatrist had also spoken at length with Nick – once or twice a week as she did with me. And she knew what kind of background he came from. One of abuse. One with little hope. And very little potential for a successful future comparable to mine. My parents would not be pleased with a match between us. If we were to become seriously involved, it might lead to a pregnancy that led to a life of failure and misery for me. The psychiatrist did not see us as a successful potential couple. So she discouraged the match at every possible chance.

But we leaned on each other in our difficult and lonely time in the rehab center with no other friends or family around to support us. We shared conversations about life, books, and how we both got to be there. We spoke of my Anglo-Indian ethnicity and what it was like for me to grow up as an Anglo-Indian in a culture. We spoke about my family and how we siblings had been given many privileges to choose our career paths.

Nick admired the family I had come from and wished he had the enormous support like I did growing up. In a few months, we became more than acquaintances.

Nick opened up to me as we sat around the outdoor area of the rehabilitation center, sometimes joking about some of the staff that worked there to break up the tension of the seriousness of his childhood. Nick especially liked to imitate that awful psychiatrist that had warned me away from him.

I became intrigued with Nick's family background. In comparison, I had been spoiled. Been given everything I'd ever wanted. I'd had to rebel to be bad. But Nick's own parents had deserted him and forced him to be bad. He'd been punished if he wasn't.

Nick grew up in a rough neighborhood. He lived in an area called Frankston, a Melbourne suburb considered 'bad' by Victorian standards. Born February 17, 1986, Nick never had a stable family. Screams were frequently heard coming from his house. Neighbors complained and the Department of Human Services, children's protective services in Australia, visited a number of times. When Nick was twelve, they ran out of patience. Even though his parents were still together, DHS made the decision that Nick was no longer safe in their care and sent him to a foster home. From that time on, Nick, the oldest of five children, never again lived with his family. Instead, he was shuffled, as is often the case with foster children, from home to home, seven in all, until he graduated out of the system at 18.

It was a blessing for Nick, in a way. He doesn't recollect his parents ever having held jobs. Instead, they lived off of government support. That wasn't, however, enough to keep such a large family – a family of seven – fed, clothed, and sheltered. So his father sought other means. Illegal means. And he would force Nicholas to assist him.

Literally, if Nick didn't comply, Keith would beat him. Rhonda couldn't interfere. She couldn't even speak out against Keith, or she would be beaten too. Keith had no qualms about beating women or children. He was an evil man.

Being the eldest, it was Nick's 'job' to finish off whatever task Keith couldn't – or wouldn't. Breaking into cars, pick pocketing strangers – whatever sick, random, and always illegal thing Keith decided to use that particular day to add to the coffers.

Even meals were regimented. They were given a strict twenty minutes to complete their dinner. If it wasn't eaten at that time, it was taken away, and the children were left to starve until the next meal was served.

So it was God's protection when Nick left, even in the loneliness of foster homes. He never looked back to try to contact his immediate family.

Nick experienced a sad and painful upbringing. He never experienced parental love. Not from Keith and Rhonda and certainly not from any of his foster homes. There, he was considered an orphan by the other children of the household and always treated as an outsider, never as one of the family.

Turning 18 meant freedom. He was no longer considered a minor and he was able to move out on his own. He rented shared houses and worked in common jobs like laborer, bartender, and retail sales rep.

Only twice did friends come to visit Nick in the rehabilitation center. Two friends that he introduced to me. They looked at each other warily. I noted the smell of weed on their slovenly clothes. And their racist upbringing couldn't get them past my skin colour - that is, not being White. So I knew Nick's friends didn't make up the whole world and suggested that he drop or disregard them like his past.

Chapter 27

My Siblings- Charisma & Calvin

But as for me, I shall sing of Your strength;
Yes, I shall joyfully sing of Your loving kindness in the
morning, For You have been my stronghold
And a refuge on the day of my distress. O my strength, I
will sing praises to You;
For God is my stronghold, the God who shows me loving
kindness. —Psalm 59:16 - 17

"For a few seconds, it got louder and faster, and the alarm changed pitch....All I saw was the brightest light I heard the loudest beep before it all had come to a sudden halt. My oxygen levels had normalized, and blood pressure stabilized."

Charisma

- A compelling attractiveness or charm that can inspire devotion in others.

Davina – Divine – supremely good or heavenly.

And so Charisma Davina has been to my parents.

My mother longed for another child. But it is with such a longing that it is often most difficult for a woman to conceive. She was

35 at the time, another strike against her. They had heard of the Divine Retreat Center and the miracles wrought there.

Perhaps…just perhaps, such a miracle could be waiting for them. And one, also, for their ill son.

The trip was always onerous. Trains and buses and the heat and traffic. But at last, they arrived for their week-long stay at the Retreat. Nine miraculous months later, Charisma Davina Dixon was born in September of 1997. She is 11 years younger than I am.

Parents from India are usually strict with their first child. Particularly if that child is a girl. Less so with the second child. By then, they have realized the child will not break, shatter upon impact with the slightest bump or bruise. The child will survive a small mistake. In fact, a child must be allowed to make some mistakes in order to learn and grow. Ahh…but not the first child. That child must be *perfect*.

But Charisma, the lucky girl, the youngest sibling, was child number three. Things were much looser for her than I…poor me. I say this with a bit of an ironic smile. How much easier my life might have been had I been the third child. But I would not have gone on to achieve all that I have achieved. To fulfill my destiny. And Charisma would not have fulfilled hers.

Singing was her destiny. At just nine years old, she began singing at church. She was known for her exquisite vocals and, over the years, became even more known for them. While Calvin had become the regular accompanist for the church music, he worked side by side with Charisma to create beautiful choir music every Sunday.

Every musician for every genre has their own success story. Some may have climbed the ladders of success early and others may have faced rejection at an early age, but my siblings were fortunate to have my father's financial support in order to pursue their music.

It was a long road for both my brother and sister that led to progression in their career. My brother went from singing at mass every Sunday to moving interstate to pursue his music career further by studying for a sound engineering degree.

As teenagers, both my siblings made decisions that were relevant to their future at that time which was producing and creating music videos in major capital cities around the country, where my sister was the lead singer.

Calvin, who developed his skills on the synthesizer in the church, had become quite a genius on the keyboard. He played and practiced for long hours. He created and produced gospel music alongside Charisma. A couple of the songs he composed and produced were played on YouTube. "Healing Rain," was a song about my accident. The Christian Rock Pop song features Charisma and recreates the scene of my accident with the news report being broadcast over it before the singing begins.

Calvin is a very focused individual who used his energy to dedicate himself to learning more about music and the way it was produced. He placed his greatest efforts profoundly, which shaped opportunities to move forward.

It was mostly his motivation to study hard so he could correlate his dreams and make them work effectively.

Those dreams and aspirations, in turn, depended on his talent, which was hugely experienced by his love for music, and he eventually moved to the United States of America.

Moving from New York to Los Angeles is the quintessential popular dream and that's what they did. Both Calvin and Charisma migrated to the land of success and worked with the nation's favorite collaborators.

L.A sure seems like a wonderland of opportunity but simply being in the city wasn't enough to guarantee their success. The music industry is a fast-paced, hungry industry and if one is not prepared to work hard, then the investment will not pay off.

So from struggle to persistence, they looked for opportunities and found their feet and a sense of their own creative compass in Los Angeles, California.

Chapter 28

My Mother and Sister Arrive

Here, for this third time, I am ready to come to you, and I will not be a burden to you; for I do not seek what is yours, but you; for children are not responsible to save up for their parents, but parents for their children.
—2 Corinthians 12:14

"I still have flashbacks of this magical celestial experience and it has been 15 years since my accident.

I had a sense of connectedness to all creation as well as a sense of overwhelming feeling of pure joy."

Their Arrival

My mother and Charisma were set to arrive on the 5th of April. It had been 51 days since my accident. It felt like forever to me. The days in rehab had been exhausting. Thank God for Nick. He was my only friend.

At first, my mother disapproved of Nick and me being just friends, as her motherly intuition knew we were going to be more than just 'friends.'

Naturally, she had concerns. What if it became serious? Would her daughter give up her education and her purpose to be here in this country all for a blue-eyed Australian boy? *That* was not what she wanted for her baby girl. Especially not when she had come so close to losing her for good.

But my mother is a practical woman. And Nick was my *first* boyfriend as far as she was concerned. She did not know about those hurried little romances I had snuck out of the house for, dodged my brother to indulge in. She didn't understand Nick's allure because I didn't have to have anyone's permission.

She convinced herself that there in the rehabilitation center, Nick could not be anything more than a friend except in my head. That he would remain just an acquaintance.

When I had a little room, I would think better of things. I would realize that the professionals were right – it wasn't a good idea to have a relationship with another head injury patient. It would be difficult enough to deal with my own trauma.

My mother was able to stay with me from the start of April until the end of June. So she was with me when the university called to notify me they would be deferring my start date to next year, as they knew I had experienced a traumatic accident – and I would need more time to recover mentally and physically.

"Because of the severity of the traumatic head injury you sustained, you cannot return until next year. You can resume your degree in February 2008. The stress of university all year round is too much for a brain in your condition. Reasoning and concentration as required in University study are just too much too soon, especially after a Traumatic Brain Injury. Problem-solving, managing the campus, it will all cause entirely too much anxiety and pressure," said the chairman at Monash University.

He continued, "we don't want you to feel overwhelmed by returning to your studies too soon. All University students feel pressure and heightened anxiety. For you, it will be compounded by your recovery from your accident. Even though you may feel fully recovered, the emotional trauma will linger for months or years."

I felt anxious, agitated, disappointed and depressed for a few days after hearing what he had to say. No one in my family agreed with him as they believed I had been completely healed. I felt like another year would be wasted if I didn't jump back in this year when I felt fully capable of going back to study.

I longed to return to University right away – July of that same year – just a few months away. And I became determined to make it happen. My will was strong. When I want something, I find a way to make it happen. Just as when I wanted desperately to pass my 10th - and then excel in my 12th - year exams. And I did. I wanted to go abroad to study and I made that happen too. Now all I wanted was to resume University immediately and I was determined to make it happen.

The way I would describe myself, I am a tenacious individual that will do whatever it takes to accomplish my goal. I worked on developing a resilient mindset that was going to help me push through my present challenge. It's like I had this unstoppable momentum that guided me towards the attainment of my goal.

So, I spoke back and forth with the University chairman for weeks and with the head of the enrollment section, who dealt with returning students. He wouldn't budge from his decision. I submitted paperwork to the university that I was making significant improvement and told them that I really wanted to begin studying next semester-July.

After my persistence and my perseverance and constant disagreement, I voiced my opinions and why I thought I should return. Thus, I was able to convince him, and then he/they succumbed to my predicament.

They then finally proposed that I only study two subjects for the first semester when I returned in July. Though we were meant to study four units per semester to see how I performed. If I did well, then I could take on a full study load the following semester.

I willingly agreed to those conditions and began studying in July 2007 – the same year that I had had a horrific accident with a traumatic brain injury that had left me in a coma and had me declared brain dead.

Becoming a Couple – It's Official

Nick and I had been talking for a month or so when we discussed the idea of 'dating,' it was Nick's idea to give it a go and we did.

I always wondered what it would be like to be in a relationship without having to get my parent's consent, as they were far away and I was now kind of old enough to make my own decisions. Having just turned 20 a few months before my accident should be considered old enough-ish. Maybe, or it could be. Don't know. Honestly, I was never really old enough in my parents' eyes.

As I dwelled on the idea that I could now maybe have a real *boyfriend* without my brother looking over my every move and tattling, it was pleasantly satisfying.

Chapter 29

Nick's Family Life

You know that I have not hesitated to preach anything that would be helpful to you but have taught you publicly and from house to house. —Acts 20:20

"People who have visited heaven offer different descriptions. Some say there were butterflies, others say there were rainbows. But for me it was the angelic beings and it's serenity that took my breath away and of course that one on one brief encounter with my Lord".

Nick's Story

Even after all those years, Nick's mother remained cold-hearted. I remember an incident sometime during the first two years Nick and I were together. With quite a bit of coaxing, I talked him into showing me where he had lived with his parents and siblings. He finally agreed and drove down to Frankston to show me. He only gave in to my request because he knew his father wouldn't be around.

He had parked on the side of the road. We looked down on the eerie house. His mother still lived there and some of his siblings as well.

Nick decided to go and say hello first before he introduced me, so he ended up knocking on the door. When his mother, Rhonda, opened it, she stared at him blankly for a few minutes. Finally, she asked, "Can I help you?

"It's Nick," he replied, disappointed she hadn't recognized her own son.

After his reply, she just stood there for a moment and abruptly asked him, "what do you want?". Confused at her response, he just nodded his head in disgust and turned around to walk back towards the car. It didn't take her long to slam the front door after receiving no reply.

Nick came back to the car, turned to me, and said, "Please don't ever ask me to ever come here again!"

I was mortified at a mother's reaction towards her eldest and promised I would never resurface his childhood nightmares. This incident reminded Nick of the callousness and abuse of the family he'd come from.

So from then on, we both moved past his family topic.

In all those years I had known Nick, his family never really reached out to him – except his grandmother, his father's foster mother. About a year after Nick's accident, she obtained his contact information through a mate of his and would contact him regularly, just to check in.

Officially, she was Keith's adopted mother as she couldn't have children of her own. Even when he was a child, she hadn't been fond of Keith. Their relationship had only grown worse as he'd grown into a hateful man. On occasion, Keith, Nick's father, would take his family to visit her until Nick was taken away by DHS (Department of Human Services). After that, they only visited their grandmother if they needed financial assistance.

Following Nick's horrible experience with Rhonda, we decided to visit his 89-year-old grandmother in Phillip Island. When I met her for the first time, we got along as if they'd known each other forever. She was absolutely lovely to Nick and me. She retold us stories about their family life.

Sadly, in 2009, shortly after our first visit, she passed away and I was fortunate enough to meet at least one valuable family member from my husband's side.

Through the years that we've been together, Nick has seen how close my family has been, how they love, share and support one another through thick and thin. He's seen our spiritual bond and our togetherness. He never experienced any kind of love or support of that kind from either his parents or his foster parents.

Nick's life turned around when he met me, for the better, I would say. We supported each other through ups and downs, hardships and struggles and mostly been through it all as a couple.

Though Nick had been baptized a Catholic, he never really understood what it meant and never practiced his faith. I couldn't blame him as he had had no guidance the way I had. As we spent our life together, I gave him that guidance that he lacked all his life.

All truth be told; initially, my family resisted Nick. They judged him by his family background and his lack of education. They didn't see any good qualities in his soul; they didn't see his strong work ethic, his upstanding morals the way I did. Eventually, they accepted us as a couple and gave us the utmost support.

It was pretty obvious my parents were always overprotective of me, wanting me to have what they considered 'the best' and to find a soulmate with the same passions, a similar career path, and financial stability that any parent would want for their child.

But I had chosen someone with a different career path to mine and someone whose goals did not align with mine and thank God I hadn't. Only because Nick was the humblest boyfriend of the lot, a simpler boy who was down to earth and someone who was willing to make something of what he did have – integrity, love, dedication.

Chapter 30

Resuming My University

Do not be anxious about anything, but in everything by prayer and supplication with thanksgiving let your requests be made known to God. And the peace of God, which surpasses all understanding, will guard your hearts and your minds in Christ Jesus —Phil 4:6

"My accident happened in Feburary 2007 and in 2008, a neurosurgeon by the name of Dr. Eben Alexander contracted bacterial meningitis and spent a week in a coma, during which time he says he took a trip through the afterlife. His description of heaven was seeing "...a gateway realm with a beautiful idyllic valley, butterfly wings, and angelic choirs, with lots of spiritual beauty, but with earth-like features."

Alas! Back To University

As my mother was able to stay until the end of June. That gave me time to help me settle into living on campus. We were able to explore Melbourne after I got out of rehab on April 17. We went to malls and sightseeing destinations. As my mother wanted me to familiarize myself with the new campus. My head still wasn't quite right and she wanted me to be comfortable in my surroundings, so we visited campus often.

I moved into the dormitory area with three apartment blocks. Three more were on the other end opposite the flats. There were some dorms that housed only boys and some that housed only girls because some students were really orthodox and couldn't live coed though there was such housing available. I lived in an all-girls flat that consisted of five bedrooms and two bathrooms with a common lounge area adjacent to a kitchen. My first-day friend, Devi, lived there too.

The following semester, I was able to take five units of study. We were allowed to take an extra unit every semester in order to catch up if a student had failed or missed out like I had.

I won't pretend it was easy. It was difficult to be away from home and my immediate family members. I was in a foreign country, starting from scratch. I got homesick at times and sometimes, I became depressed or stressed with the workload as the professionals predicted I might. But to cope, I stayed back after hours. I frequently communicated by email to my lecturers with my queries and assignment-related work. I questioned myself now and then, feeling anxious as to my capabilities. But I always came back to this: "I came here for a purpose. I came to study to achieve a degree when youth like myself were not as fortunate to study abroad. I am lucky to be here." With that, I never gave up. The first six months were the hardest. But having Nick there made a huge difference. He supported and encouraged me to get past the hardship and focus on the outcome. He understood because he was struggling to cope with his own trauma.

If I felt I couldn't cope, I meditated and prayed novenas to help me overcome my struggle. I marched on in the light of the Lord. Sometimes I visited the university chaplain, Glenda, whom I got to know very well over the years. She would pray with me when I visited her on campus.

I was grateful to my parents for sending me there and allowing me to continue studying in the country where I had almost died. It took a lot of courage and faith. And their surrender to the Heavens.

I lived on campus for the first eight months – so I wouldn't have to travel to get there -experiencing university life. I enjoyed it – the late-night study sessions, the crazy party scenes, the trips to new places I'd never seen before.

Eventually, I moved into a shared accommodation not too far away. I experienced a whole lot of life.

Having come from such an exquisite childhood, I was used to having so much done for me. University life was just the opposite, especially after I moved off campus to a shared house. For my first degree, I studied for a Bachelor's in Communication, majoring in journalism. I worked as a waitress as a side job for a bit in an Italian restaurant close to the university, where I earned about $200 a week.

I thought that was pretty good for a newcomer.

Onward Ever Onward

During the years I worked towards my Bachelor's degree at the university, I struggled both financially and emotionally. Like many college kids, there were days when, after paying my rent, I couldn't afford to buy food, but I did not ask my parents. As my parents had paid such a large amount for my education already. International students paid $10,500 per semester with two semesters per year. It felt entirely too selfish to ask them to give me any further financial help when I knew my brother and sister needed financial support for their music careers too.

For the three years it took to earn my bachelor's and the two to earn my master's, I moved around the suburbs, renting rooms until I finally bought my own house. I tutored students from grades 3 to 12 on the side. I earned $25 to $30 per hour teaching them English, Geography, History, and Legal studies in their homes.

I preferred tutoring 15 hours a week to waitressing, so I quit working at the restaurant.

I was terrified to drive since the accident, so I took public transport to get anywhere. It took me an hour or two to get to my destination when it would have only taken twenty minutes by car. Often, I would be out past dawn. I crossed unsafe areas just to earn a bit of money, lucky not to be attacked. I sat in deserted train stations waiting for the next train, and walked to remote bus stops without a soul in sight. How did I go unscathed?

I believe we all have guardian angels, and of course, I repeated Psalm 91 every single day without fail. They are meant to protect and watch over us. According to Christian tradition, every one of us has a guardian angel who accompanies us from the moment we're born until the moment of our death and stays at our side every moment of our lives. Mine was surely watching over me as I stood quietly waiting in the dark and lonely nights for a bus running late.

I also traveled most of Australia to complete internships for reputable newspapers and magazines for my first two journalistic degrees – Cosmopolitan and Marie Claire as well as some smaller publishing companies. I also worked for some small radio companies. I traveled interstate to Sydney for the internships and stayed in hotels for a week or two. I struggled financially, physically, and emotionally. Yet, I enjoyed this part of my life more than the years when I was so pampered because I gained my independence, and it made me more determined as an individual and mentally stronger.

I also struggled emotionally as I tried to adapt to the university timeline of submitting my assignments and studying for exams. The demands of studying and meeting deadlines while balancing work and life weighed on me, but I managed to accomplish my goals.

I graduated with a Bachelor's and continued studying for a Master's in Communication. Soon after, I began an honors degree and then pursued a doctoral (Ph.D). Not long after, I finally learned how to drive; hence I would then commute to work and university by car.

Philippians 4:13- I can do all things through Christ who strengthens me.

Chapter 31

Our Christian Holidays

Therefore let us keep the Festival, not with the old bread leavened with malice and wickedness, but with the unleavened bread of sincerity and truth —1 Corinthians 5:8

"Carol Meyers at the age of 60 had a near death experience and her description of heaven was, "as I was standing there, this incredible peace overtook me. There were no more earthly emotional holes in my spirit. I was completely whole. It was an incredible feeling. This state of being is no doubt part of the scripture that there will be no tears or sorrow in Heaven".

My Christmas's

Each December, during the university holidays, I would fly home to enjoy Christmas for six weeks to be with my family and dog, Casper. Although Calcutta winters are cold, we never had a snowy Christmas.

Christmas is my favorite holiday of the year. Preparing for Christmas was the best part of the year – even better, to me, than Christmas day. I loved seeing the shiny Christmas lights decorating our tree and our house.

From the first day of December, all the way up to Christmas Day, we would listen to Christmas carols while my mother prepared her delicious Christmas cakes. Young carolers came to the door to get us in the Christmas spirit. And my mother made cakes with dried fruits, almonds, raisins, and pistas along with sweet curled Anglo-Indian fried treats called Kalkals mixed with flour, sugar, and butter. She baked us cookies as well.

On Christmas Day, I woke up with a huge smile on my face, my heart full of joy, and my stomach rumbling. I could smell all the spices of the cooking in the whole building where we lived. As soon as I got out of bed, I would rush to the Christmas tree to open up my gifts.

It was always a busy morning as we attended morning mass at St. Thomas's Church at 10:30 am. When we returned from mass, our extended family – cousins and all –usually came over and we had the different types of Anglo-Indian dishes to eat called vindaloo, Kofta curry (meatballs), flavored rice, salad, and some other dishes as well.

Ash Wednesday's Back Home

Ash Wednesday is an auspicious day on the Catholic calendar. It is the day that begins when we Catholics go to mass and the priest touches our forehead, making the sign of the cross with ash. He says, "Remember that you are dust, and to dust you shall return." The ash symbolizes the dust from which God made us and is a solemn reminder of human mortality and the need for reconciliation with God. It marks the beginning of the penitential Lenten season, which is observed with abstinence and fasting for the 40 days leading up to Easter Sunday – the Day Jesus rose from the dead.

My parents would not eat meat for these 40 days. My brother and I skipped this abstinence initially and I began practicing it in

Australia every year instead as I was considered old enough to do so and still do.

Good Fridays in Calcutta

The Friday before Easter Sunday is a time of adoration, spent meditating on Christ's sacrifice of love for the salvation of souls in preparation for the joy of Easter. As students of a Catholic school, we would get roughly a week of holiday in anticipation of this holiday and, as part of the celebration, our family observed abstinence – no food or drink except water until 5 o'clock for anyone over the age of 14. That rather put my brother and me out of sorts. Charisma was young enough to escape the difficult fasting presented.

Our Good Friday started in the morning at 6:30 am. We would walk to seven churches. The tradition of visiting seven churches on Holy Thursday probably originated in Rome. After the Mass of the Lord's Supper, early pilgrims visited the seven basilicas as penance to pray before the Blessed Sacrament in each church ending at the tombs of Saints Peter and Paul.

After the Mass of the Lord's Supper, in which Christians remember Jesus Christ's last meal with his Apostles on the night that he was arrested, followers then remember Jesus's Agony in the Garden as follows: after the mass, the main and most of the side altars are stripped. All crosses are either removed or covered. The Blessed Sacrament is placed in the tabernacle on the Altar of Repose, and churches are open for silent adoration. All of this is in response to Jesus' request to his apostles according to the **Gospel of Matthew 26:40,** *Could you not, then, watch one hour with me?*

We would finish walking to all seven churches by 10 am, then would rest or have a nap before mass and drink plenty of water to stay hydrated, as it is usually the time of the year when India has its summer approaching.

So around 2:30 pm, we would attend the Agony mass. My brother and I were in agony attending the mass because we hadn't eaten all day.

The Three Hours Agony, also known as the Tre Ore, the Great Three Hours, or Three Hours Devotion, is a Christian service held in many Roman Catholic, Lutheran, Anglican, and Methodist churches on Good Friday. It is held from noon until 3 pm to commemorate the three hours that Jesus Christ hung on the cross. The service presents the seven last words of Christ, though they are, in fact, the sentences that he spoke as he died upon the cross.

The first is *"Father, forgive them, for they know not what they do."* — **Luke 23:34** Though terrible cruelty and injustice are being done to him, he is begging forgiveness for those who are crucifying him, he is seeking compassion and even in his death is giving his love. His purpose remains *"the Son of Man has come to seek and to save the lost."* **Luke 19:9 - 10**

The second: *"Today you shall be with me in Paradise."* **Luke 23:43**

He is promising that even those sinners left behind will be able to join him in a better place beyond this world, though the place he calls 'paradise, may not be heaven itself. It is certainly a safe place along the way. The sure hope of the righteous Lord and of those made righteous through him is that death does not separate the righteous from God.

The third: *"Woman behold thy son, Behold thy mother."* John 19:26, 27

As John tells us, *"Jesus, knowing that his hour had come to depart out of this world to the Father, having loved his own who were in the world, he loved them to the end"* John 13:1. And in this declaration, he is declaring his special love for his mother and the disciple into whose care he gave her.

The fourth: *"My God! My God! Why has Thou forsaken Me?"* Matthew 27:46

This declaration of our Lord Jesus Christ causes us to recall Psalm 68, *"And I looked for one that would grieve together with me, but there was none: and for one that would comfort me, and I found none." None. Not even God, Himself, allowed comfort to God, Himself! The paradox of all paradoxes – how could we ever comprehend this?*

The fifth: *"I am thirsty."* John 19:28

It is one of the Christian beliefs that we come to our "salvation through suffering," as Jesus endured his suffering for us upon the cross and thus brings man to the glory of God.

The sixth: *"It is finished."* John 19:30

His life. His ordeal. What he started. What God started.

The seventh: *"Father, into your hands, I commend my spirit."* Luke 23:46

Jesus had *"humbled himself by becoming obedient to the point of death, even death on a cross"* Philippians 2:8 With one last cry, Jesus yields up his spirit, humbly bows his head in total submission, and commits his body and soul up to God.

Mass finished just before 5 pm when we rushed home to eat like ravenous scavengers.

My mother or the cook lady would whip up the meal for us which did not include meat on Good Fridays because it was forbidden. It was mashed eggplant mixed with onions and chilies, fried potatoes (a very common dish in India), pulses and beans as a gravy called Dal in Hindi, plain white rice, and a salad. This is a traditional Good Friday meal for our family.

Holy Saturday was for solemn prayer and again, no meat, only vegetarian food, which might include fried Indian cottage cheese (called paneer).

When Sunday arrived, we prepared for 10:30 am mass, after which we returned home for an eagerly awaited lunch that my mother prepared buffet-style and, at last, the meal included meat. She would cook chicken dishes, too, because I refused to eat any other type of meat.

Bandel Church

We would regularly go to The Basilica of the Holy Rosary, another pilgrimage destination (commonly known as Bandel Church). It is one of the oldest Christian churches in West Bengal, India. Founded in 1599 and situated in Bandel, Hooghly district, this prominent historical parish church is a memorial to the Portuguese settlement in Bengal.

Part of the Roman Catholic Archdiocese of Calcutta, it was considered miraculous because Jesus' Mother Mary was believed to bring miracles to those who believed and came to worship at this place. A primary attraction of the church is the statue of Mother Mary located in a niche near the top of the fasçade. We would regularly travel the two hours it took us to get there on a Saturday or Sunday to spend a few hours in prayer and attending mass. We packed a lunch of sandwiches to eat on the way or when we arrived.

The Basilica of the Holy Rosary was built in 1599 by the Augustinian Friars who were spreading Christianity to the Dutch, British, French, and then Portuguese settlers. It is dedicated to Nossa Senhora do Rosário, Our Lady of the Rosary. The Rosary is a Prayer of Hope – Symbolic of the Roman Catholic veneration of Mother Mary.

When Moghal forces under Sha Jahan attacked and destroyed the church, they killed all of the Friars except Father Joan Da Cruze, who tried to save the statue of Mary. He gave it to one of his followers, Tiago, whom he instructed to swim it across the Hooghly River to safety, but Tiago was shot through with Mughal arrows and the statue sank to the bottom of the river.

Though the church was rebuilt, the statue was thought to be lost forever. One night, Father Joan Da Cruz saw lights coming from the river and was drawn by sounds. He heard the voice of Tiago saying, "Our Lady." The next morning, a local fisherman told the priest that "Giri Maa," the blessed mother, had come back. To his surprise, Father Joan found a cross and the lost statue on the field. People have come to the place wishing for miracles ever since. They light candles to Our Lady of Good Voyage and ask for their prayers to be answered.

I hated the journey to and from Bandel because there were many more homeless people sleeping on the side of the road and more street dogs wandering about.

Sometimes they got hit because the highway had big trucks and buses that rarely stopped for animals, particularly dogs, that crossed the roads and just ran right over them. It is a harsh reality in most 3rd world countries where this sort of animal cruelty is a fact of life.

When we arrived there and because the journey took over an hour, our families would carry snacks and lunch. We often made a day out of the trip and usually ate after our prayers. We would attend mass, pray at alternate statues and kneel up a flight of stairs, reach the altar at the very top, put our petitions in the box, kiss the statues and sometimes visit the parish priest.

Chapter 32

Life- Few Years
after the Accident

And above all these put on love, which binds everything together in perfect harmony. **—Colossians 3:14**

Have you ever wondered whether your dog is able to sense spirits or pick up an undetectable phenomenon? Well, my dog Casper sensed something on the day of my accident when he refused to go into my dark bedroom and barked at nothing visible at 1am (Indian Standard Time)...he sensed something out of the ordinary.

First Comes Love - Engaged

Nick was the first boyfriend I had without Calvin looking over my shoulder, with the freedom to make my own choices, without worrying about getting back home by a certain hour of the night so my parents wouldn't catch me.

As our relationship progressed, it felt more real. We got to know each other more, to see each other often even though we lived separately. Nick allowed me to focus on my studies and encouraged me so much when I felt down. He boosted my confidence with pep talks about how lucky I was to be given this opportunity and how blessed I was to have a family that supported me.

It was during this time that I started to introduce Nick more to my spirituality. I took him to church and we began praying together. I taught him to pray the rosary. We would recite the rosary when we met up and after we moved in together.

After our engagement, Nick and I shared a house with other roommates. It was a place near to the university. I continued my studies while he worked. In 2011, I urged him to take an IT course, a year-long course in networking and software. He worked in a casino as a blackjack dealer while he studied. When he earned his diploma and went to work in computers, he found that he loved it.

Because he loved what he did, I pushed him further to attain more qualifications in his field.

Then Comes Marriage - Our Wedding – October 16, 2011

My entire immediate family attended my wedding, although Calvin almost didn't make it. He was living in Bombay, attending a music college. A typical artist, Calvin was often preoccupied. Perhaps he was composing when he should be thinking about more worldly things, such as when his flight was leaving. Like when he was supposed to fly to Australia for my wedding, he had to catch a flight by himself – something he had rarely done.

We were all somewhat spoiled, having traveled together and having had the maids, cooks, and chauffeurs to help us organize everything.

He misread the time on the ticket and arrived at the airport at 11 pm instead of 11 am. Missing his flight, he had to forfeit the cost of the ticket and couldn't catch a flight to Melbourne until the next day.

Actually, it was a day of near misses. I, too, nearly missed my wedding. I, a stickler for punctuality, arrived twenty-five minutes late at the altar. Nick spent the night before at a family friend's house.

It was a tradition that the groom should not see the bride for three nights before the wedding. But I needed him to pick up the flowers and the cake since I still did not drive, so we could only honor one night apart.

Busy with the photographer who kept wanting to take photos as the wind blew about my gown and my hair, I got delayed. I had to bite my lip and keep posing, and in the midst of all the blissful photography, I was further delayed because my limo got stuck in traffic.

My wedding mass was held at 2 pm at a local church nearby. I arrived just before 2:30. My brilliant photographer, Andrew, wanted even more pictures…of me entering the church; I calmly obliged as I knew this was a once-in-a-lifetime event.

My father stood outside, ready to escort me to the altar where my husband-to-be waited for me.

After mass, we rushed around again, this time taking pictures of all sorts before we had to jump back in the limo to head to the heart of the city, where my reception was being held. Everyone made their way to Port Melbourne as soon as possible as my lavish event was held on a boat, and of course, I didn't want the boat to leave without them.

The boat only had a capacity of 50 people and it truly was a unique experience. The boat was docked in a rich suburb called the Docklands and it was a 3.5-hour reception/ tour of the spectacular city. We sailed under bridges to stunning views of the open sea. Though it was a small reception, it was still memorable and a once-in-a-lifetime opportunity.

Our onboard ceremony included an officiant announcer, a DJ, a buffet and beverage package along with a magnificent view.

I took the opportunity to gratefully make a toast to my parents for their support. By then, even my husband knew that I worshiped them both. My father had saved me with his miraculous prayers. My mother had seen me comfortably ensconced and back in university. I shed a few tears while I raised my glass of champagne in their praises.

Then Comes Babies - The Children

Nate – *Hebrew.* God has given. (My firstborn)

Christian – *Latin.* Follower of Christ, from the word 'Christianity.' (My second born)

I was 29 years and 11 months old when my first son, Nate, was born on the 2nd of November 2016. The 2nd of November is all souls day in Roman Catholicism; it is a day that we Catholics commemorate all the faithfully departed, those baptized Christians who are believed to be in purgatory. Purgatory is believed to be a place where those souls who are not yet saved because of their actions on earth. So it is the 2nd of November that we are in constant prayer for the souls of the departed.

Because of my solidarity and the importance of Catholicism, Nate is fortunate to have a mass offered in every continent due to this day.

Christian was born on March the 23rd though his due date was the 26th, in 2018. Christian was born during Lent. What is Lent? You may ask.

It is a season that consists of 40 days of prayer and fasting along with almsgiving that begins with Ash Wednesday and concludes at sundown on Holy Thursday (3 days before Easter), where we Catholics enter a more deep devoured mystery of Christ's passion.

In 325CE, it was a time of preparation of candidates for baptism and a time of penance for grievous sinners who were excluded from Communion and were preparing for their restoration. As a sign of their penitence, they wore sackcloth and were sprinkled with ashes. This form of public penance began to die out in the 9th century, and it became customary for all the faithful to be reminded of the need for penitence by receiving an imposition of ashes on their foreheads on the first day of Lent—hence the name Ash Wednesday.[1]

I consider myself really lucky and blessed as both my children were born on auspicious days in the Catholic Calendar.

Chapter 33

The Present

I will praise you as long as I live, and in your name I will lift up my hands. —Psalm 64:4

"It was not an ordinary dream, and it wasn't really a 'dream'-dream;

I felt so peaceful in his presence, so calm. It was like I wasn't the least afraid or scared."

And I instantly felt this extraordinary peace, serenity, coming over my whole being. There was an understanding on a deeper level and an understanding that I had never experienced before. Whatever his plan was, I simply just had to trust it and trust HIM."

I remained friends with Devi until I finished my Bachelor's degree, even after she returned to Bangladesh for a few years. She then came back to Melbourne soon after. This time she brought her son and husband too. We did meet up and reminisced on the old times.

* * *

Jesus said, "Did I not tell you that if you believe, you will see the glory of God" **John 11:40**

Miracles happen every day. Belief, prayer, and faith can change everything – anything. A moment changed my life. But my father's faith brought me back from death's doorstep. Doctors – not one, but many – declared me brain dead and told my family to tell me 'goodbye,' to prepare for my death, or at the very least, to prepare for me to never recover, to remain in a vegetative state. Yet, here I am, whole, well sound and telling you my story.

I returned to university shortly after a horrific accident. Just five months after being hit by a sedan plowing into me at 80 km per hour. Brain dead, my skull rushed blood. My lung punctured. My pelvis fractured. Yet, miraculously, I recovered in 9 days and my memory went back to normal a few weeks after.

It can be done. Believe and pray. The Lord God is with you.

Jesus said to her, "Daughter, your faith has healed you. Go in peace and be freed from your suffering." **Mark 5:34**

Let this story be your inspiration. Let it guide you in your walk with the Lord, in encouraging you to ever have faith in the Lord. Pray and He shall listen.

"Many are called, but few are chosen." (Matthew 22:14)

Bibliography

1. A. J. Wallace, R. D. Rusk, *Moral Transformation: The Original Christian Paradigm of Salvation* (New Zealand: Bridgehead, 2011),

2. Alban Butler and Paul Burns, 2005, *Butler's Lives of the Saints*, Burns and Oats. ISBN 0-86012-383-9. p. 251.

3. Amy Tikkanen, 2016, *"Roman Catholic-Life of Mother Teresa"*-The Editors of Encyclopedia Britannica (Retrieved 25 May 2009)

4. *Blessed Are You: Mother Teresa and the Beatitudes*, ed. by Eileen Egan and Kathleen Egan, O.S.B., MJF Books: New York, 1992

5. Carey, W. H. (1882). 1882 – The Good Old Days of Honourable: "East India Company | Definition, History, & Facts | Britannica".(Retrieved 17 October 1998)

6. "Calcutta Archdiocese : HOWRAH & HOOGLY DEANERY". *The Roman Catholic Archdiocese of Calcutta.* (Retrieved 2014-08-26)

7. *Catechism of the Catholic Church No. 1992.* Vatican City-State. Justification is conferred in Baptism, the sacrament of faith. Christian Faith Publishing

8. "Canonisation of Mother Teresa – September 4th". *Diocese of Killala.* September 2016. Archived from the original on 8 September 2016. (Retrieved 4 September 2016)

9. Chisholm, Hugh, ed. (1911). "Penance" . *Encyclopædia Britannica.* Vol. 21 (11th ed.). Cambridge University Press 2

10. Cotton, H.E.A., *Calcutta Old and New*, 1909/1980, pp 820-821, General Printers and Publishers Pvt. Ltd.

11. Corbett L. *The Religious Function of the Psyche.* London: Routledge; 1996. (Retrieved 12 January 1997)

12. Dady, Dorothy S. (2007). *Scattered Seeds: The Diaspora of the Anglo-Indians* Pagoda Press -7

13. Giacino, J. T., Ashwal, S., Childs, N., Cranford, R., Jennett, B., Katz, D. I., ... Zasler, N. D. (2002). The minimally conscious state: definition and diagnostic criteria. *Neurology. 58,* 349-53.

14. Gillian Weyant, 2011, *'The life of saint Faustina'*-The mystical humanity of Christ publishing

    Hackett, Conrad (December 2011). "Global Christianity A Report on the Size and Distribution of the World's Christian Population Census" . Pew–Templeton global religious futures project. pp. 19, 27

15. John Paul Kirkham, 2019, 'A Simple Guide to Catholic Faith', John Paul Kirkham

16. Kay T, Harrington DE, Adams R, Andersen T, Berrol S, Cicerone K, et al. Definition of mild traumatic brain injury. J Head Trauma Rehabil. 1993;8(3):86–7

17. Laureys S, Celesia GG, Cohadon F, Lavrijsen J, León-Carrión J, Sannita WG, Sazbon L, Schmutzhard E, von Wild KR, Zeman A, Dolce G; European Task Force on Disorders of Consciousness. Unresponsive wakefulness syndrome: a new name for the vegetative state or apallic syndrome. BMC Med. 2010 Nov 1;8:68. doi: 10.1186/1741-7015-8-68.

18. Lovell MR, Iverson GL, Collins MW, McKeag D, Maroon JC. Does loss of consciousness predict neuropsychological decrements after concussion. Clin J Sport Med. 1999;9(4):193–9.

19. National Assessment Program". ACARA. Archived from the original on 3 March 2016. (Retrieved 4 March 2016)

20. Nicholas J. Santoro (2011). *Mary In Our Life: Atlas of the Names and Titles of Mary, the Mother of Jesus, and Their Place In Marian Devotion.* iUniverse. pp. 379–380. ISBN 978-1-4620-4022-3.

21. *The Diary of Saint Maria Faustina Kowalska: Divine Mercy In My Soul,* Saint Faustina Kowalska, 2003, Marian Press. ISBN 1-59614-110-7 (Note 96).

22. *The Diary of Saint Maria Faustina Kowalska: Divine Mercy In My Soul*, Saint Faustina Kowalska, 2002, Marians of the Immaculate Conception (Notebook I, items 10 and 11). https://www.thedivinemercy.org/message/devotions/pray-the-chaplet ref 10

23. The Holy Bible: King James Version. (2011). Hendrickson (Original work published 1611)

24. Wu, Margaret (2015). "What National Testing Data Can Tell Us". In Lingard, Bob; Thompson, Greg; Sellar, Sam (eds.). *National Testing in Schools: An Australian Assessmen*t